THE
DREAMING
KIND

SHORT STORIES AND FANTASIES

CRITICS PRAISE C. S. FRIEDMAN

"Friedman has always been notable for the complex quirky detail work that makes her worlds fascinatingly memorable places to visit."
— *Locus*

"Friedman writes cogently on the nature of human desire for knowledge, and the dangerous covenants necessary to attain it."
— *Publisher's Weekly*

"In many ways, C. S. Friedman's work reminds me of William Gibson's—unique settlings, complex and fascinating (though not always likeable) characters, cool ideas and technology, a smart and savvy style."
— *Fantasy Literature*

"Here are Ms. Friedman's usual virtues: plenty of action, brisk pacing, and characters and settings painted with broad strokes and vivid colors."
— *Booklist*

"Truly one of the great voices of speculative fiction...the sheer imaginative genius, not to mention incredible power, of Ms. Friedman's formidable storytelling gift is indescribable—you simply have to experience it."
— *Romantic Times*

"Epic fantasy with a keen, dark edge...shows off Friedman's gift of craft and authorial insight."
— *South Bend Tribune*

"A gifted storyteller and an innovative creator."
— *Library Journal*

BOOKS BY C. S. FRIEDMAN

THE MADNESS SEASON
IN CONQUEST BORN
THE WILDING

The Outworlds
THIS ALIEN SHORE
THIS VIRTUAL NIGHT

The Coldfire Trilogy
BLACK SUN RISING
WHEN TRUE NIGHT FALLS
CROWN OF SHADOWS
DOMINION *(Prequel novella)*

The Magister Trilogy
FEAST OF SOULS
WINGS OF WRATH
LEGACY OF KINGS

The Dreamwalker Chronicles
DREAMWALKER
DREAMSEEKER
DREAMWEAVER

THE ERCIYES FRAGMENTS *(White Wolf RPG)*

THE DREAMING KIND *(Short Stories)*

THE DREAMING KIND

SHORT STORIES AND FANTASIES

BY

C. S. FRIEDMAN

Tridac Publishing
Sterling, Virgnia
2021

ISBN: 978-1-7371619-1-2

Dedicated to David Huffman-Walddon,

For all the years of love and support.

ACKNOWLEDGEMENTS

Special thanks to Kim Dobson, Larry Friedman, Casey Gordon, Linda Gilbert, Carl Cipra, Jon Goff, David Williams, Jennifer Hina, David Huffman-Walddon, and Zsuzsy. I couldn't have done it without you guys!

CONTENTS

INTRODUCTION

When I first discovered speculative fiction, it was through short stories. Isaac Asimov, Brian Aldiss, Richard Matheson, Robert Sheckley, Phillip K. Dick, and the early writings of Robert Silverberg enthralled me. This was the literature of "What if?" in its purest form: ideas conjured, presented succinctly, and then left to percolate in the reader's mind.

Most of my own writing has been focused on novels, but every now and then an idea occurs to me that calls for a different kind of voice, and a short story is thus born. The book you hold in your hand contains seven such stories, as well as an eighth that was…well, let us say it was written in response to a challenge that had interesting results. A few minor editorial changes have been made. I've added several poems to the collection, excerpts from two of my novels, THIS VIRTUAL NIGHT and IN CONQUEST BORN, and a selection from THE ERCIYES FRAGMENTS, courtesy of Paradox Interactive AB.

I hope you enjoy reading these short works as much as I enjoyed writing them. If you'd like to share your thoughts with me, you can reach me through the contact link on my web page, https://www.csfriedman.com/contacts/, or on Facebook. I love to hear from readers!

Celia S. Friedman
Sterling, Virginia

PERFECT DAY

When Stanley Betterman awoke Monday morning, he did not know that everyone else in the world was naked.

His own pajamas were securely in place when his brainware buzzed his neural centers, cutting short a particularly nice dream about falling mortgage rates. The striped cotton might have looked a little more greenish than usual as he staggered to the bathroom, but his Color My World app always took a little while to get up to speed in the morning. Otherwise, there was no sign that anything was wrong.

The image that stared back at him from the mirror was the same one he saw every morning: a nondescript man with a remarkable lack of noteworthy features, flanked by two columns of biological readouts that seemed to float in mid-air. Checking the numbers, he saw that his blood pressure, cholesterol and blood sugar readings were all within acceptable limits, but his HDL was a little low. No doubt his Positive Health Habits app would let him know what he needed to do to correct that.

Still unaware that the act of wearing clothes made him an anomaly on Earth, Stanley scrubbed his teeth until they gleamed, then let his bathroom scanner point out the bits of plaque he'd missed. CONGRATULATIONS! his brainware projected when he was done, bright red caps scrolling across his field of vision as a trumpet fanfare blared in his ears. YOU GOT IT ALL! The accolade made his head hurt, but running the Positive Reinforcement Suite earned him a 2% discount on his health insurance, and with work going the way it was, he needed to save every cent that he could. Maybe if things picked up later in the year, he could purchase a deluxe display that would be less intrusive. Supposedly there was one with the Hallelujah Chorus where you could actually adjust the volume.

When he was done getting washed and dressed for work, he checked his Time Management app, which gave him a 72% efficiency rating for the morning's hygienics. It was one of his lowest scores that month. Maybe if he'd brushed his teeth more effectively he could have scored higher. There was no penalty for a low rating, but Stanley took pride in his efficiency. Perhaps he should seek some hygienics counseling.

DID YOU TURN OFF THE LIGHTS? his Tenant Safety app demanded as he left the room. DID YOU UNPLUG ALL HAZARDOUS APPLIANCES?

He was heading toward the kitchen when he passed his older brother in the hall. At first his brain didn't register the fact that the man was completely naked. When it did, Stanley just averted his eyes and walked on. His brother's Progressive Lifestyle app sometimes prompted him to do strange things, and Stanley didn't want to be judgmental.

But when he entered the kitchen, he saw that all the other members of his family were naked as well. He stood in the doorway for a moment and blinked, trying to come to terms with that.

His mother turned and smiled at him; he blushed and looked away.

"Eggs this morning?" she asked. "I got a good deal on modified yolks."

He nodded dully and sat down, trying not to look at anyone.

He'd moved back in with his family a year ago, during the last economic crash. Normally it wasn't too bad. Everyone was running the Home Alone app, which told you where the other members of your household were located at all times, so that you could avoid them. (*Next best thing to being alone!* the ad proclaimed.) But they had taken to eating breakfast together so that they would have a chance to group-sync the app. If you didn't do that once a week it could go out of phase, and then you might find yourself wandering into a room that you expected to be empty, only to find someone already in it. Highly irritating.

"Eggs are fine," he said, staring down at the table.

"You okay?" his naked older brother asked.

"I'm okay," he mumbled.

"You don't look okay."

It was bad etiquette to discuss brainware problems at the table, but obviously his brother wasn't going to leave him alone. "I think I have a virus," Stanley said. "I'll deal with it at work."

"Is it the nudie virt?" his naked 14-year-old brother demanded.

"Geoffrey!" his naked mother exclaimed

"What's a nudie virt?" the older brother asked.

"Malicious virtual program," the 14-year-old explained. "Hit the social networks late last night. Makes everyone around you look stark naked." He giggled. "I hear the President caught it."

"Is that true?" Stanley's mother frowned as she positioned a dishrag strategically in front of her chest.

"It's not a big problem," he muttered, trying not to look at her. (Also trying not to think about what the Vice-President would look like naked.) "I'll just run a neurocleaner when I get to work."

She put down a plate of Safe Eggs in front of him. He picked up the salt shaker and shook it over the plate. 30 MG SODIUM, his brainware informed him. 60. 90. The numbers scrolled higher and higher as he continued to shake. Then: WARNING! Bright red letters rushed across his field of vision. RECOMMENDED SODIUM LEVELS FOR THIS MEAL HAVE BEEN EXCEEDED. TERMINATE FLAVORING IMMEDIATELY!

Suddenly he felt a wave of defiance come over him. His ancestors in the American Revolution had risked their lives to defend their personal freedom; surely he could do no less! Defiantly he continued to salt his food, oblivious to the fact that he had exceeded his own taste parameters for scrambled eggs. Sometimes you had to make a personal sacrifice in the name of freedom.

WARNING! A loud buzzer sounded in his ear. YOU HAVE EXCEEDED YOUR RECOMMENDED DAILY SODIUM LIMIT! ONE BHC POINT HAS BEEN ASSIGNED TO YOUR ACCOUNT!

Cursing under his breath, Stanley put the shaker down. In his mad bid for freedom he had totally forgotten about the behavioral clause in his medical insurance. Now he had a Bad Health Choice point on his Health Maintenance record for the month. Four more of them and his premiums would go up. Damn.

It's the fault of the nudie virt, he told himself. Trying to eat breakfast without looking at anyone was driving him crazy.

He finished as quickly as he could, and managed to get out of the house without any more embarrassing voyeurism. His car was waiting for him.

"Direct, scenic, or budget mode?" it asked.

"Budget", he responded, as he did every morning.

The car started its engine as he entered, shut its doors, and began to roll. Glancing out the window, he noticed that some of the people on the street now had flickering outlines of clothing surrounding them. Evidently his brainware's Security Suite was clearing the virt out of his system on its own.

Today the car took him on a roundabout route that looped past an ad strip, slowing down so that he would have time to read the densely packed billboards flanking the road. When they reached the end of the strip his car surprised him by driving him to another one, even longer than the first. Usually Budget Mode only required one stop, but advertisers were getting greedier these days. Annoying though it was, he couldn't afford to do without the fuel subsidy he got for agreeing to participate in an ad immersion program.

But slowing down for the second ad strip made him late for work. He texted his apology to his boss as he entered the building, choosing the appropriate excuse from a checklist. YOUR EXCUSE IS ACKNOWLEDGED, came the answer. THIS MONTH'S ATTENDANCE RATING: 78.21%. PROTECT YOUR PAY RATE BY ARRIVING ON TIME.

As he hurried to the elevator, he decided that an environmental virt might soothe his nerves. He chose one called *Rain Forest*

Fantasy, and a moment later the interior of his building appeared to be filled with leafy green ferns, towering trees, and brightly colored birds. But there must have been a glitch in the app, because more and more birds kept appearing, until hundreds of parrots and toucans and macaws were watching his every move. By the time he got to the elevator he was beginning to feel like he was in a Hitchcock movie, so he switched off the virt as he stepped inside. The real world would have to do.

His office was freshly painted and nicely furnished, and its large faux-window was running a Living Nature app. He uploaded a view of the Grand Canyon with midday lighting, and watched as a group of tourists made their way down into the sunlit crevasse. It was important that his office be attractive enough that customers didn't feel they had to run virts while they were talking to him. There was nothing more frustrating than trying to discuss mortgage points with someone who was watching a horde of drunken Vikings ravage Saxon women on your desk.

Stanley's first customer was a wizened old Hispanic man who wanted to buy a house for his grandson. His credit was sound but his advanced age set off warning bells, so Stanley put in a request for his medical records. There were several conditions that could increase a man's risk rating, in which case a customer might still get his mortgage, but the interest rate would be higher. Someone who didn't take good care of himself was less likely to keep up with his loan payments.

But this customer had a clean medical record, and Stanley's Emotoscan app, which had been analyzing the man's body language since his arrival, assigned him an Estimated Emotional Stability Rating of 86.2. That was well within acceptable parameters, so Stanley signed off on the loan.

His next customer was a tall black man wearing an African medallion around his neck. His skin was very dark.

"Good day," he said. "I am Ngoto Mbege, first cousin to the exiled prince of Nigeria. I have come to you for a loan, it being to restore accounts that were hidden from sight during recent revolution. An assistance of American is needed—"

The door suddenly slammed open and half a dozen men rushed in. They were wearing body armor labeled MAKAFI and carrying automatic weapons. Stanley was startled at first, but then he saw the bright red 'V' on their helmets. Makafi Security was very careful about labeling its virtual products so people didn't get confused.

"Leave this office!" one of the security virts barked. The Nigerian did not move fast enough, so all six of them grabbed him and forced him into a steel box which had suddenly appeared by the door. When he was safely locked inside it, one of the soldiers saluted Stanley. "He won't be able to bother you now, sir. Do you want him disposed of?"

Stanley nodded, and the malvirt flickered out of existence along with its container. The Makafi team followed.

Stanley frowned. There was way too much malware in his head today. Maybe he should visit a neuropractor after work. He had his brainware provide a local directory, and he called a neuropractor whose office was only a few blocks away. The receptionist asked for permission to access his credit record for the last ten years, and after running a detailed analysis of his medical payment habits, she agreed to give him an appointment. (She was a real person, of course; no patient would be expected to share that kind of personal information with a machine.)

The nudie virt tried to relaunch itself several times that afternoon; evidently Stanley's Security Suite hadn't been able to fully uninstall it. He was forced to purchase a malware detection upgrade, which instructed him to shut down all his other apps while it scoured his system. Apparently it found something problematic, and he had to function without his brainware for most of the afternoon. By the end of the day he had developed a pounding headache…but everyone in the world still had clothes on, so at least that was something.

While walking to the neuropractor's office, he refused an offer to earn extra fuel points by accepting an advertising detour. But an underwear ad flashed briefly in front of him as he crossed the street, and he sighed; evidently his pop-in protection was on the blitz as well.

The neuropractor looked over all his systems and then said that the problem was that he was running a thousand different programs to deal with bits and pieces of his digital health, rather than addressing the greater whole. Stanley didn't understand all the details of that, but he knew that his customary approach had not worked, so he agreed to try a round of 'data stimulation therapy.' Apparently that involved a lot of residual virts being stimulated, and he spent an hour having to relive sounds and images he thought he'd deleted long ago. The worst was a disco remix of Beethoven's Fifth Symphony that he vaguely remembered having loaded one night in college when he was drunk. No wonder his brainware was having so many problems; it had to wend its way through a lifetime of garbage data every time it needed to process something.

Stanley wasn't sure whether he felt any better when the therapy was over, but the neuropractor's scanner assured him that he did, and since he was no longer being accosted by virtual ads, maybe it was true.

By the time he got home, Stanley could feel the strain of a long day catching up with him. He consulted his Home Alone app to locate any other family members who were in the house. To his annoyance, he saw that there were already people in the living room, den, and office. The only room besides his own bedroom that was currently unoccupied was a small storage room in the basement.

With a sigh he headed downstairs. The room was filled with half-open boxes, but by rearranging some of them he managed to clear enough space to sit down. As he opened his e-Book app his Call Center chimed and informed him that he had a call.

"Yes?" he said aloud.

"Hey, Stan." The virtual voice was that of a co-worker, Jeff Simmons. "A bunch of us are heading over to Riley's for drinks. You want to join us?"

Tired as he was, it was a very tempting invitation. He still had a few alcohol credits left for the month, so he could enjoy a couple of beers without it impacting his health insurance premium.

"Sure," he said. "I'll come right over."

He shut down the e-Book app and struggled to his feet. But before he could get to the door a message from his Positive Reinforcement Suite appeared in front of his him: WARNING! ENERGY LEVELS

SUB-OPTIMUM. ANTICIPATED ONSET OF FATIGUE: 8:45 PM. EARLY RETIREMENT RECOMMENDED.

Stanley hesitated. It was 8:15 already. If he went to the bar now he'd hardly have time to enjoy himself before he became tired. But if instead he chose to go to sleep early, he would earn two Good Health Choice points. That could help offset the egg-salting fiasco.

With a sigh he sat back down on his box, yawning as he opened his e-book app once again. His health program had been right; he was already starting to feel tired. But a good night's sleep would fix that. His Positive Reinforcement Suite had inspired him to make the right choices all day, his neuropractor had cleared all the annoying kinks out of his brainware, and his Sweet Dreams app would make sure that he slept deeply and had pleasant dreams. He would certainly feel better in the morning.

As he chose a book to read, he wondered briefly what things had been like before the digital age. What utter chaos life must have been! He was fortunate to have been born in the time and place that he had, with so many modern conveniences at his beck and call.

With a sigh of satisfaction he settled back in his tiny cardboard nook, called up the series of virtual advertisements that was required by his reading material, and waited for the moment when his ad quota for the day would finally be satisfied and he could enjoy his book.

AUTHOR'S NOTE *for* PERFECT DAY

Written in three days as a lark, "Perfect Day" was first published in the MAGAZINE OF FANTASY AND SCIENCE FICTION. To my surprise, it turned out to be my most critically acclaimed short story. David Hartwell included it in his collection of YEAR'S BEST SF 18, and it was assigned reading in a hospital-sponsored seminar on Medical Ethics.

Those who have read my novels will recognize a few technological gadgets that also appear in my Outworlds novels. (THIS ALIEN SHORE and THIS VIRTUAL NIGHT.)

DOWNTIME

By the time the messenger from the DFO came, Marian had almost forgotten about the Order. You could do that if you tried hard enough. You just tucked the unwanted thought deep into some backwater recess of your mind until the normal clutter of everyday life obscured it, then you pretended it wasn't there. Marian was good at that. She had her own special places for hiding things, dark little crevices in her soul where one might tuck a fact, an experience, or even a whole relationship, so that it never saw the light of day again.

She knew the day her sister died that a lot of new things were going to have to go in there, and she'd done her damnedest to make them all fit. She'd done so well, in fact, that when the doorbell first chimed, there was a brief moment when she genuinely didn't know what it was about. Who would be coming to see her in the middle of the day? She was curled up with her children and her pets at the time: two boys, a girl, two cats, and a small dog, whom she collectively referred to as "the menagerie". They couldn't all fit on the couch at one time, but they were trying. Only Amy had given up, and she knelt by the coffee table now with her crayons laid out before her like the brushes of a master artist, her face screwed tight with concentration as she tried to draw a horse *exactly* right. When you're the oldest child, you have to do things right; the other children depend on you. Marian watched her delicate blonde curls sweep down over the paper for a moment before trying to disentangle herself from the others. With five bodies and two afghans involved it wasn't easy, and finally she yelled out "Coming!" at the top of her lungs, hoping that whoever was on the other side of the door would hear her and wait.

The dog didn't come with her to the door. Maybe that was an omen. Usually he was the first one there, to welcome strangers. But dogs can sense when things are wrong, sometimes even when their owners don't. Marian walked past him, ignoring the complaints of both cats and children as she looked through the peephole to see who was there. It was a woman, neatly coifed and with the socially acceptable minimum of makeup, wearing some kind of uniform, holding a letter in one hand and an electronic tablet in the other. That was odd. People didn't get many real paper letters these days, unless it was something important. For a moment Marian couldn't think of who would have sent her such a thing…and then memory stirred in its hiding place. She was suddenly afraid. She hesitated a moment before unlocking the door, but couldn't give herself a good reason for not doing so. Trouble doesn't go away if you refuse to sign for it, does it? As she opened the door, Marian noted that the woman's uniform didn't have any insignia on it. That could be just an oversight, or it could indicate that whoever had designed the uniform believed that people wouldn't open the door if they knew what she was there for. Not a good sign.

The woman looked up at Marian, down at her tablet, then up again. "Marian Stiller?"

Marian could feel all the color drain from her face as she stared at the woman. Maybe she should lie about who she was, and say that Ms. Stiller wasn't home. Shut the door, lock the problem outside, and stuff this memory down into that dark place with all the others. That would buy her a bit more time. But what would it really accomplish? Sooner or later they'd find her, and then there would be fines to deal with on top of all the rest. Maybe even jail time. The government was notoriously intolerant when it came to people who tried to avoid their filial duties.

"I'm…I'm Marian Stiller."

The woman glanced at her tablet again, as if checking her notes.

"This letter is for you, Ms. Stiller." She handed her the envelope, thick and heavy. Marian took it numbly and waited. "I'll need you to sign for it, please." The pad was given to her. Marian hesitated, then pressed her thumb onto its surface. The thing hummed for a moment, no doubt comparing her print to government records. *Confirmed*, it blinked at last. The woman took it back from her, cleared her throat, and then assumed a more formal position that she clearly associated with official announcements.

"Ms. Stiller, I have delivered to you an Order of Filial Obligation. You are required to read the contents and respond to them in a timely manner. If you do not respond, you may be subject to fines and/or imprisonment. Do you understand?"

She barely whispered it. "Yes, I understand."

"Do you have any questions?"

"Not in front of the children." She was acutely aware of them not far away, and heard for the first time how their chatter had quieted suddenly. They had to be protected from this. That was her first job. As for questions...the Department had places for questions to be answered. Later.

"I understand." The woman bowed her head a token amount. There was no sign of emotion in her expression or in her posture. What did it feel like, to spend your day delivering messages like this? "Good day, then." Was she one of the people who believed in the Filial Obligation Act, who thought it was a good thing? Marian didn't ask. She didn't want to know.

She watched her walk away from the house, because that was one more thing to do before opening the letter. When the woman had rounded a corner and that excuse was gone, she turned with a sigh and shut the door behind her. The envelope was heavy in her hand. The room seemed unnaturally quiet.

"What? What is it?" She met the eyes of child after child, all gazing up at her with the same worried intensity as the dog in its corner. Children, like animals, could sometimes sense trouble. She looked at the letter in her hand and forced herself to adopt the teasing tone she used when they worried over nothing. "It's just mail. You've never seen paper mail before? I swear!" She shook her head with mock amazement and curled up on the couch again. She couldn't read it here, not in front of them, and she certainly couldn't go off to a private room now that they were watching her. She threw the letter onto the far end of the coffee table, face down so that they wouldn't see the DFO insignia next to the address. It landed on top of a pile of drawings, covering over the lower part of a horse. Amy fussed at her until she moved it. By that time everyone else was arranged properly on the couch once more, so she found some cartoons on the children's net, and she turned up the volume and hoped it would distract them. Best to just pretend the letter wasn't really important, until they forgot about it. Then she could go off to the bathroom alone with it, or say she had to start cooking dinner, or…something.

She wondered if they could hear how hard her heart was beating.

* * *

To Ms. Marian S. Stiller, child of Rosalinde Stiller:

This Order of Filial Obligation is to inform you that your family status has been reviewed, and it has been determined the debt formerly assigned to Cassandra Stiller is now the rightful debt in whole of Marian S. Stiller, only surviving child of Rosalie Stiller.

Enclosed you will find an Appraisal of Filial Debt and Order of Obligation from our office. Please review both these documents carefully. You are expected to comply with this Order by the date indicated. Any questions you have should be addressed to our office within that time frame. Failure to comply with this Order promptly and with full cooperation may result in substantial fines and/or imprisonment.

* * *

She was helping Amy with a jigsaw puzzle when Steve came home, teaching her how to analyze the shapes with her eyes so that she didn't have to try as many wrong pieces before she found the right ones. The boys had tried to help, but they didn't have the attention span to keep up with it, and they had gone off to play with the dog.

She almost didn't hear him arrive. Then Amy squealed happily and ran to greet him, and Marian looked up. His broad smile of homecoming wavered a bit when he met her eyes, as if he was seeing something there that he didn't know how to interpret.

Amy hugged him joyfully, but as he lifted her up to his chest for loving return squeeze, his expression said to Marian, *What's wrong?*

She shook her head and glanced at Amy. He understood.

The ritual of homecoming always took a while, but today he kept it as short as he could, and she was grateful for that. She needed him a lot more right now than the children did, and certainly more than the pets did.

When he was done with all the requisite greetings, she whispered some excuse to the children, and she led Steve into their bedroom. Not until he had shut the door behind them did she draw out the envelope that she'd hidden in the nightstand and hand it to him.

He glanced at the DFO insignia on the envelope and his eyes narrowed slightly. She watched as he pulled out the letter and read it, then the forms. It seemed to her that he read everything twice, or maybe he was just taking his time with it. Scrutinizing every word.

Finally he looked up at her and said quietly, ''You knew this was coming.''

She wrapped her arms around herself. Fear was starting to set in, and she didn't want him to see how bad it was.With a sigh he dropped the pile of papers down on the bed and came over to her. She was stiff when his arms first went around her, but then fear gave way to a need for comfort, and she relaxed against him, trembling. She'd been trying not to think about the Order all day, but now…seeing him read it made it more frightening, somehow. More real.

"You've been lucky," he said softly. "Cassie's taken care of this for years. How many people get a judgment like that? Normally both of you would have been involved from the start. Now she's gone, and you're the only child left…it was only a matter of time, Mari."

"I know, 1 know, but…*" I'd hoped it would never come to this,* she wanted to say. What terrible words those were! He'd think she meant that her mother should have died already, when what she really meant was…something less concrete. Something about wishing the world would change before it sucked her down into this, or at least the law would change, or…something.

'I don't know if I can go through with this," she whispered.

His arms about her tightened. "I know, honey. It's a scary thing." But did he really know? His parents had died in an accident when he was young, before Time technology was anything more than a few theoretical scribbles on a scientist's napkin. Long before something like the Filial Obligation Act was even being discussed, much less voted on by Congress. She found that she was trembling violently, and couldn't seem to stop. The government had just announced it was going to take away part of her life. It would never do that to him. How could he possibly know what that felt like?

She heard him sigh, like he did when he saw her hurting and didn't know how to help. "Look, we'll go down to the DFO and talk to one of their counselors, all right? Maybe there's some way to…I don't know...appeal the terms of the Appraisal. Or something."

Or help you come to terms with it. The words went unspoken.

"All right," she whispered. It meant she could put off the matter for another day, at least. Pretend there was some way out of it, for a few precious hours.

That night she dreamed of her mother.

* * *

"Frankly, I find the whole thing just wrong." Her mother whipped eggs as she spoke, the rhythm of her strokes not wavering even as her eyes narrowed slightly in disapproval. "We have children because we want them, and we take care of them because we love them, not…not …" She poured the eggs into a bowl with an exasperated sigh. "Not because we expect something in return."

"Do you think it's going to pass Congress?" Marian asked.

"I don't know." She picked up a handful of diced onions and dropped them into the bowl. "I hope not. The day we start 'paying'

*parents for their services is the day...well, that will say a lot about
how much is wrong with our society, won't it?"*

* * *

The state offices of the DFO were on Main Street, in an old
building that had once been the county courthouse. Marion's eyes
narrowed as she studied the place, first from the outside, then while
passing through its great double doors. You expected something
associated with modern science to be in a building that was...well,
modern. Gleaming sterile floors instead of ancient hardwood,
claustrophobic cubicles instead of scarred wooden desks. Something
that made visual sense. This was all wrong.

Or maybe anything would have seemed wrong today.

She paused in the outer lobby, where approved vendors were
allowed to showcase their wares, and Steve waited quietly beside her.
The vast bank of brochures against one wall seemed more appropriate
for a tourist resort than a government office, and the brochures
themselves were likewise colorful and sunny, promising services in
perky catchphrases that were meant to make the alien seem
reasonable. *Give your parents the Time of their lives and have more
time for your own!* That one was from a travel agency which
specialized in Time-intensive vacations, on the theory that people
might be willing to accept less Time if the quality of the experience
was outstanding. *Wonder where your Time is going?* Another
beckoned. That one promised peace of mind in the form of special
investigative services, which would track your parent's actions and
provide a complete report when you...when you...well, when you
could read it. And *Time after Time* offered counselors for parents, to
help them organize the fragments of their second life into a
meaningful whole.

Suddenly she felt sick inside. Steve must have seen it in her face,
for he whispered, "Shhh, it's all right," and quietly took her hand.

It wasn't all right. It wasn't going to become all right, either. But
she'd be damned if she'd start crying about it all over again, least of
all here. "I'm okay." Wiping some moisture from her eyes, she

nodded toward the door to the DFO office. He took the hint and opened it for her. Sometimes little things like that helped. Just little signs that you weren't alone in all this. Thank God he had been willing to come down here with her.

The wait was long, but the office seemed well-organized and things were kept moving. Most of the people waiting were sitting in a common area reading brochures, or whispering fearful questions to their spouses, siblings, or friends. A few were just staring into space, like children who know they're going to be given some unpleasant medicine, and there's no way to get out of it. Most of them seemed to be holding numbers, spit out from a machine as ancient as the building itself, and small plastic pails near each of the desks were full of the little paper tabs.

She registered at the main desk, telling the receptionist that she had an appointment for Appraisal adjustment, then got a number and took a seat to wait. Steve just held her hand and waited with her. There wasn't anything more he could do to help, and they both knew it, but it was good to have him there.

After some time her number was called and they were ushered into a small office in the back of the building. The counselor greeted them with a smile that seemed genuinely warm, though surely it was no more than a professional courtesy. How could you do a job like this all day and keep smiling to the end of it? She was a small black woman with threads of silver overlaying the tight jet braids of her hair, and Marian guessed her to be about 50. Too old to be doing Time, if there was an alternative, and still too young to be needing it. The lines of her face bore witness to a caring nature, and Marian felt a spark of hope in her chest.

"I'm Madeline Francis," the woman said, and she had the kind of voice which seemed pleasant no matter what the subject matter was. "Please have a seat." She indicated a pair of chairs facing the desk, and while they sat down she looked over the files on Marian's case. "It seems to me everything is in order," she said at last. "Why don't you tell me what you're here for?"

"I'd like my Appraisal reconsidered," Marian said. She could feel her hands starting to tremble as she said the words, and wrapped them tightly about the arms of the chair so that it wouldn't show. What she really wanted was for this whole nightmare to be over, the Order rescinded, and her life back to normal. But she knew she wasn't going to get all that, not if she asked for it outright. Indirectly...well, one could still hope.

A finger tap on the computer screen brought up the Appraisal. "6.4. You're the only surviving child, yes? That's not a very high number, considering."

It's 6.4% of my life! She wanted to scream the words, to rage, to cry...but instead she just gripped the arms of her chair more tightly, until her knuckles were bloodless. "There are...circumstances."

The black woman raised an eyebrow and waited.

"I'm the primary caregiver for three children. Young children. Steve's job takes him out of the state a lot, and while he's gone I'm the only one there for them."

Stever nodded. "We never let strangers care for them." But was that argument of any value here? Marian couldn't read the counselor's face at all. "To lose parenting two days a month at this time in their lives could affect their development."

"Ms. Stiller." The counselor's voice was soft but firm. "There are millions of families in this country who employ caregiver assistance. Most of them aren't even doing it for Time, merely to gain the freedom they need to take care of life's necessities. If you don't have relatives who can help out, then I'm sure in the coming months you can find someone to hire." She held up a hand to forestall the next objection. "Let me ask you a few questions, if l may. All right?"

Marian hesitated, then nodded. Where were all the neat arguments she'd prepared for this meeting? All the proper words? She couldn't seem to find them.

"Did you have a good childhood, Ms. Stiller?"

She hesitated. ''That's hard to answer. There were good times and bad times—"

"Of course, of course. Perfectly normal. But overall, do you feel that you and Cassandra got the attention you deserved? Were your parents there for you when you needed them?"

"I guess...yes." She knew the answer was the wrong one to give, but she didn't want to lie outright. This woman had all her files, and probably Cassie's testimonies as well. She'd know.

For one dizzying moment she wished that her mother had been more distant, more harsh, so that she'd have some more concrete complaints to offer to this woman, something that would justify a lesser Appraisal. Then her face flushed with shame for even thinking that.

"She was a full-time caregiver also, wasn't she? Rare in that age." The woman's eyes met Marian's and held them. Warm eyes, caring eyes, but with a core of self-confidence and conviction that no easy argument would shake. "You appreciated that, even at the time. Enough so that when your own children were born you decided to raise them the same way. Isn't that right, Ms. Stiller?"

She whispered it. "Yes. But…" Nothing. There was nothing to say. She twisted her hands in her lap as she listened, knowing the battle was already lost. Feeling sick inside.

"She was there for you when you were sick, wasn't she? And when your sister was in a car accident and needed physical therapy to get back on her feet again, didn't your mother take care of all that herself?"

"I don't know. I was away at college then."

"Your mother took a class in physical therapy at the local college, just to be able to help Cassandra herself. So that strangers wouldn't have to do it." She glanced at the computer screen for a moment, her expression softening. "Your sister appreciated that a lot, Ms. Stiller. She attributed her complete recovery to the attention she got back then. To the fact that your mother put aside her own life for a time, to take care of her. She never protested her Appraisal, did you know that? Or the fact that the initial Order assigned Time to her alone, and didn't divide it up between the two of you."

Her voice was a whisper. "She was much closer to our mother than I was."

"Recently, perhaps." She glanced at the monitor. ''About how long would you say that's been the case, Ms. Stiller? How long since you've, say, visited your mother on a regular basis?"

Marian looked down, unable to meet the woman's eyes. "A few

years. Maybe. . .two."

"Maybe five?"

She didn't say anything. Five years ago was when Cassie had started doing Time. Mom hadn't needed Marian much after that...or so it had seemed.

"Did you know she had a second stroke?" the woman asked.

Marian nodded, still not meeting her eyes. "It was a small one."

"When your life is already reduced, even a 'small one' whittles away a precious portion of it." Softly, she said, "The doctors don't think she'll live much longer. A few years at most. You know that, too, don't you?"

She said nothing.

The counselor leaned forward on her desk, her hands steepled before her. "I'm going to be honest with you, Ms. Stiller. You could appeal this thing, if you wanted. I don't think any judge in this country would alter the Appraisal for you, but you could tie it up in litigation if you wanted, long enough to gain some time. The law's still new enough for that. Maybe if you tried hard enough you could even delay judgment until there wasn't an issue any more. You understand me?"

She felt a flush rise to her face as she nodded.

"I don't think you're the kind of person who would do that, Ms. Stiller. I think in your own way you care about your mother, as much as your sister did. You're just a bit scared, that's all." She sat back in her chair; the steepled fingers spread out flat onto the desk's surface. ''That's only human. It's a scary technology."

"That's not it," she whispered. But there was no conviction in her voice this time.

"We grow up in our bodies, regard them as a natural part of who we are. Mind, soul, flesh, it's all part of one unified entity. Then suddenly science comes along and makes us question that neat little package. What would happen if you could separate mind from body? What would that make us? The thing is, after all the questioning, it turns out the answer hasn't changed. We are who we are, and even this scary little bit of technology can't really break up the package." She paused for a moment, her dark eyes fixed on Marian, studying her. How many times had she given this pep talk? What cues was she looking for, that would tell her how to proceed? ''Anything else is just an illusion, Ms. Stiller. You know that, don't you? A very precious illusion, for those whose own bodies have failed them."

"Yes," she whispered. "But..." Marian had prepared a thousand words, but now she couldn't seem to find any of them. Was it just fear she felt, anxiety about a technology that seemed to belong more in science fiction than in her real life? Or was there a shadow of selfishness there as well, something she should feel guilty about?

The woman gave her time to speak, and when she did not, finally said, "Ms. Stiller, I want you to do something for me."

The words startled her out of her reverie. "What?"

"I want you to go see your mother. Not for Time, just a visit. You haven't seen her since this Order was assigned. Tell me you'll do that. Just visit with her. And then, if you want...come back here and we'll talk about the Appraisal. Or we can arrange for counseling for you, if you feel that's what you need." She paused. "All right?"

She drew in a deep breath, trembling, and said the words because they had to be said. "All right."

The woman offered her something. A business card. Marian gave it her thumbprint, and heard it hum as it sent the woman's contact information to her account.

High technology. What a blessing.

"Thank you," she whispered. Not because she felt any gratitude, but because...that's what you said when a meeting was over. Wasn't it?

Her husband led her out.

* * *

Amy was having trouble with arithmetic. Little wonder, since she'd rather play with her crayons than work with the computer to memorize her numbers. Marian had printed up flash cards on paper, using one of Amy's drawings on the backs. The girl was fascinated by them, and had to be told at least three times about how flash cards used to be in every house, way back before computers, before she would settle down to work.

It was good to do such little things, if only as a distraction. Marian would have liked to think that she could lose herself in the task, but the sideways glances her daughter kept giving her made it clear that Amy sensed the wrongness in the air. Marian kept waiting for her to ask about it, and dreaded having to come up with an answer—any attempt at honesty would only frighten the girl, but surely she'd sense it if her mother was hiding something—yet the moment never came. Maybe Amy sensed that there were no answers to give. She'd most likely wait a day or two and then blurt out questions when they were least expected. That was her way.

That was fine with Marian. Give her a few more days, and she might be able come up with some answers.

* * *

The Home was much as she remembered it: neatly manicured lawns surrounding wide, low buildings; bowers brushing up against sunbaked bricks in carefully measured clusters; benches set along the sides of the path at precise intervals, to receive those whose legs could not sustain them. There were several people about, enjoying the morning sun, and at first she assumed they were staff. But as she passed a young woman, it suddenly occurred to her that maybe they weren't. She found herself staring at the back of the woman's head, and had to force her eyes away before others took notice. The contacts were almost invisible, she'd been told. Easily hidden beneath a full head of hair. Cassie had offered to show her what hers looked like up close, but Marian hadn't wanted to see them. Were any of these normal-looking people doing Time? She suddenly felt sick inside, and would have sat down on one of the benches if she wasn't afraid that if she did so she might never get up again.

What was she doing here? This was crazy. Even her mother had said it was crazy. Didn't that count for anything?

When she got to the receptionist's desk, she had to take a deep breath to find her voice. "I'm here to see my mother, Rosalinde Stiller."

"Ah, yes." The aide behind the desk was young, her face still beaming with the freshness of teenage enthusiasm. Too young to even understand what Time was, much less have to worry about it. "Come with me."

They'd moved her mother. Cassie hadn't told her about that. Out of the ward where cases of moderate dependency were kept, into a place where things were...worse. Marian could feel her chest tightening as she followed the aide down the sterile white corridors of the new ward. There was no pretense of normal life here, no attempt to disguise the nature of the place. It looked and felt like a place where people died. Why hadn't Cassie told her?

Because you didn't want to hear it, an inner voice whispered. *She knew that.*

"In here, Ms. Stiller." The room was small, a private one. They'd seen to that, Steve and Cassie and Marian; they'd made sure her mother had all the best things. Except that after a while...how much did it mean? She looked about at the bright curtains, fresh flowers, rolling table...anywhere but at the bed. Anywhere but where she needed to be looking.

"Are you all right, Ms. Stiller?"

Her mother was frail. So frail. She had forgotten that. Sickness robs a body not only of strength, but of substance. She remembered her mother as a bundle of strength, of energy, always restless, always moving. Always doing something. It was hard for her to reconcile that image with the woman who lay before her. Hard for her to cling to her memories, when the very source of them had become so changed.

Slowly she sat down on the edge of the bed, and took her mother's hand. The skin was strangely silken, thin to the touch, and blue veins throbbed softly beneath her fingertips. Not a hand she recognized. She looked up slowly to find blue eyes fixed on her. Clear, bright, almost strangers to the wrinkled flesh surrounding them. There was some emotion in those eyes, but Marian couldn't read what it was. The expressions she remembered from her youth were all gone, stolen away muscle by muscle, as age severed the link between mind and body. Where was her mother, inside that flesh? She gazed into the clear blue eyes with all her might, trying to make contact with the soul behind them. Did her mother feel the same sense of dislocation when she looked in a mirror? Did she wonder whose this stranger's face was, that looked so drained and pale? Surely not her own. Surely.

The counselor was wrong, she thought. *You can divorce mind from body, even when they share the same flesh.*

"She can't really speak any more." The aide spoke quietly from behind her. "With great effort, maybe a few words. No more." Marian must have looked surprised, because the nurse asked, "You didn't know?"

"No, I...no. Cassie didn't tell me."

Cassie didn't tell me a lot.

She squeezed her mother's hand as she leaned down slowly to kiss her on the forehead. This close, she could catch the scent of her familiar perfume, and she ignored the tang of medications and ointments that breezed in its wake, losing herself for a moment in the smell of the mother she remembered. Nothing like this. But the human soul doesn't fade with age, does it? Only the flesh.

It's only two days. She forced herself to digest the words, forced her soul to accept them. *Two days a month, and the rest of your life stays the same as it always was. Surely you can do that for her,* she told herself, trembling. *Surely she deserves that much.*

She would have done it for you.

* * *

Remembering: Her mother's fingers folding tissues into a neat little fan, just so, each fold perfect. Binding them around the center with another twist of tissue, tight enough to bunch the layers together. Finely manicured nails prodding the layers apart, separating each fragile ply, spreading them out carefully one after the other, until the whole is a delicate rose, fragile and perfect.

"Getting harder to do," her mother says. "My dexterity's not what it used to be; soon I won't be able to make these at all." She puts the rose down in front of Marian and indicates the pile of tissues next to it. "Now you try."

* * *

Steve insisted on coming with her. She tried to get him to stay home with the children, to let a friend take her to the Time clinic, but he wouldn't hear of it. Bless his stubborn, loving heart. He had even canceled a business trip to San Diego to make sure he could be home the day before, in case her floundering courage called for husbandly support. And it did. She wasn't crying anymore, but she spent a lot of time that day in his arms, trying to take comfort from his presence while not letting the children sense how very scared she was.

They did, though. Children were like that. Amy even picked up enough from conversations she overheard to ask if Mommy was doing Time. For a moment Marian didn't know what to say. There was no way to lie that Amy wouldn't eventually catch on to, if Marian was going to have to do Time every month. At the same time…she was too young. She wouldn't understand. She shouldn't have to understand, not at this phase in her life.

"Mommy's going to see Grandma,' she said at last. Kneeling down to meet her eye to eye, willing all the calm sincerity into her voice that she could manage. "She's going to give Grandma some Time so she can feel better."

"Will she get better then?" the child asked.

For a moment Marian couldn't speak. Finally she whispered, "Probably not, sweetheart. But this will make the sickness hurt less."

No more questions. Thank God. Maybe Amy had enough intuitive sense to understand that Marian had no more answers. Not now, anyway.

She'll ask again. The boys will grow up, and they will ask. What words will you give them, that a child can understand? Or will you put it off until it's too late, and they have to learn the truth in school, or on the street…from strangers? What will you do then?

The world has changed. You can't shield them from it forever. Later. She would deal with that later. One thing at a time…

* * *

Ms. Stiller?

Darkness. Soft darkness. Voices muted as if through cotton, distant whispers.

Are you all right, Ms. Stiller?

Were they talking to her, the cotton voices? It took her a minute to process that thought.

"I'm...I'm all right."

You're going to feel strange for a little while. That's normal. Try to relax.

"I'm trying . . ."

You understand what is happening, yes? It's all been explained to you?

Why was it so hard to think? Was that because of the drugs they had given her, or her own fear? Strange, how the fear seemed distant now. Like somebody else's emotion, a thing to be observed rather than experienced. "They told me."

A heart was beeping on a monitor nearby. Hers? She could hear it through the cotton as they spoke to her. Steady, even beeps.

It's going to feel like you're falling asleep. There may be a sense of falling away from your own body. That's just an illusion, you understand? It comes from the drugs we use. Your mind won't actually leave your body, ever.

"Body and soul, an indivisible alliance." Did she say that out loud? The drugs were making it hard to think. Where had that phrase come from, some propaganda leaflet? She couldn't remember.

That's right, Ms. Stiller. She could hear people moving around her, but she couldn't make out what they were doing. Was her heartbeat usually that slow? They had given her tranquilizers because she'd asked for them, but she'd never had drugs that felt this strange before. Pinpricks of electricity tickled her scalp. Were those the contacts they had inserted? *Body and soul are a unit, and can't be divided. What we're going to do is create an illusion that it's otherwise...but it's only that, an illusion. You're going to sleep for a little while—at least, that's what it will feel like—but you'll still be here, inside your own flesh.*

"Yes, I understand...sort of..."

Your mother will get feedback from your sensory contacts. She'll be able to send messages to the parts of your brain that control movement. But she won't actually be inside you, you understand? Just...suggesting motions, and observing the world through your senses.

The fear was a distant thing now, muted by drugs. Wonderful drugs. They could tailor emotions these days like you tailored a suit. *A bit short in the terror, be careful. Look, the dread isn't matching up right. Add some calmness to that seam, please.*

"It will be like she's in my body."

For her. Yes. One of the contacts moved a bit. Being adjusted? *For you...it will be like sleep. You may dream a bit, not whole dreams but bits and pieces. Feedback from within your brain, as your body interacts with the world. You understand?*

Thank God her friend Diane had agreed to watch the children. Thank God. One less thing to worry about, as Marian prepared to give over control of her body to someone else. Diane would know how to handle the children. She knew Marian and Steve well enough to know that while they were here, dealing with all this mad scientist machinery, they didn't want someone else explaining things to Amy and the boys. No, that was something parents should do themselves.

Marian remembered how her mother had talked about this process. She'd thought it was a bad thing. Children shouldn't owe their parents their bodies.

But you didn't know then how helpless you'd be, did you, Mom? Or how much a few borrowed hours might mean? There was a tear in her eye. She tried to reach up a hand to wipe it away, but her arm wouldn't respond to her anymore.

Her mother would have done this for her, had Marian been crippled. Would have given over her body to her child so that Marian could live a normal day. Twenty-four hours without pain, without handicaps, without weakness. Twenty-four hours in the body of a loved one. The ultimate gift.

Relax. Ms. Stiller. Calm footsteps. Heart beeps. Other sounds, hospital sounds. She tried to let go, not to listen. The cotton helped. *We're going to initiate transfer now.*

The first time is always the hardest, they'd told her. Like labor.

Yes. The second child was easier. The youngest drew rainbows. Bright colors, youthful colors. Age was gray and blue, her mother had said, cooled by time, softened about the edges. A sudden sadness filled her heart, bringing fresh tears to her eyes. She missed red, suddenly. She missed the oranges and umbers of autumn in the mountains. The trees still changed, but it wasn't the same. She knew the sunlight was gold, but it didn't *feel* gold anymore. Cassie had brought flowers to the clinic, beautiful bowers, but all the smells she remembered from her youth were gone. She wanted to smell the flowers again. Leaves like precious velvet, she wanted to touch them, to feel the golden sunlight on her face...

Why was she crying? She knew what the sunlight was like. Where was the sorrow coming from? A sudden bolt of fear lanced through her, and the steady rhythm of the heart monitor began to quicken. Someone else's thoughts—

She could feel hands upon her, but just barely. *Easy, Ms. Stiller. Easy. We're almost there.* The hands faded away, then, and with them all the sounds of the room. A soft roaring filled her ears, that seemed to have no source. She could feel herself being drawn out of her body, and she tried to fight it ...but she didn't want to fight it...soft panic wrapped in cotton, oh so distant. Someone else's panic. Someone else's body...

She drifted into Downtime slowly, never knowing when the transition took place. Just like sleep. People didn't fear sleeping, did they?

* * *

Waterfalls. Splashing on the skin, scouring body and spirit. Turning up her face up into the rain, laughing to feel it trickle into her nose. Glorious rain and a crown of strawberries. God, the smell is sweet! So many layers to savor! Redness and freshness and sweetness and tartness all mixed up together, and she can taste each one. Crimson slickness down her back, tartness frothing in the waterfall as she laughs.

Youth is gold, wonderful gold, that tastes like chocolate sprinkles on the tongue. Veins of gold altering the sunlight into speckled networks of color: yellow, orange, red, green. The colors of youth, of life. Drink in the color. Roll the orange around on your tongue. Red is pepper and spice, that stings the nose. Sunlight is chocolate. Wonderful chocolate! Waterfalls are blue, not dull aged blue but the clear blue of a cloudless sky. The water smells of strawberries as it washes away all shame and despair. Who would have thought that a simple thing could bring so much joy?

* * *

"Marian?"

She could feel the images parting like mist as she struggled toward the surface, toward consciousness. Strange images, like and unlike dreams. Where had they come from? The doctors had said that Time was no more than biological remote control, that the best of all their science could not put two minds in contact with one another directly, but Marian wasn't so sure of that any more.

''Marian?"

"Yes." She gasped the word, then opened her eyes. The clinic room slowly came into focus. ''Steve."

He squeezed her hand. The sensation helped her focus again. "You okay?"

"Yes." She drew in a deep breath, trembling, and let it out slowly. "Yes, I…think so. Is it…is it over?"

He nodded.

She managed to sit up and leaned against him, weakly. Her skin felt very fresh and clean. Her hair smelled of strawberries. Shampoo? She touched the soft strands in wonderment.

"Did you see her?" she asked him.

He shook his head as one of the nurses answered. "That's not allowed until later, Ms. Stiller. When you're both accustomed to the process, then other people can be involved. For now…only staff."

It felt strangely difficult to speak…but that was just illusion, right? Marian hadn't been permanently disconnected from anything in her body. "What did my mother…I mean…"

The nurse smiled indulgently. "What did she do, Ms. Stiller? Is that what you want to ask?"

She nodded.

The nurse picked up a tablet and tapped it until it displayed the data she wanted. "From nine AM to one PM, your mother worked with our staff to help fine-tune her contacts. Full sensory transfer was confirmed at 1:13." A smile flickered across her face. "She promptly asked us to bring her a cannoli, with chocolate sprinkles on it. All proper cannoli have chocolate sprinkles, she told us. She then took a long shower. And went for a walk in the garden. Our people accompanied her, of course. She won't be allowed to go out alone until you're both more accustomed to the transfer. According to my notes, she spent a long time searching out leaves on the ground, and holding them up to the sunlight and staring at them."

"It's autumn." Marian could hear her voice shaking as she spoke. "The colors…all the gold…" She shut her eyes and remembered the colors in her dream. The sheer joy of seeing them. *Is that what I gave you?*

"She had her usual Time dinner." The nurse smiled. "A sampler of all the salty and spicy things she's normally not allowed to eat. Nothing so bad youneed worry about it." She looked down at her notes, and her eyes narrowed in puzzlement. ''Then it says…she another shower."

Marian whispered, "I understand." *Waterfalls.*

Steve put an arm around her shoulders and squeezed gently.

That's the worst part of all, her mother had told her once. *When you can't even wash yourself. That's when you feel like it's all over, like you're not really living anymore, just waiting to die.*

She leaned against Steve and tried to be calm. It was over now, at least the first Time. So why did she want so badly to cry in his arms? There wasn't anything of her mother inside her, not anymore. Science couldn't do that. Wasn't that what they told her? Time was only an illusion. No direct mental contact was possible. No real sharing.

"Is there anything else?" Steve asked.

"Yes." The nurse went to a table by the window and picked something up. "She wanted you to have this. She said you would understand." She held it out to Marian, a small pink object that seemed to have no weight at all. It took Marian a moment to realize what it was. When she did, she took the fragile tissue flower into her hand. Every fold so perfectly made, every ply so perfectly separated. For a moment she couldn't speak, could only stare at the thing. Then she whispered, "Can I see her now?"

The nurse shook her head. "She's asleep right now, Ms. Stiller. The first Time with a new connection is always exhausting. Why don't you come back tomorrow?"

"Of course." She couldn't stop staring at the rose. "Tell her...tell her...I understand. Please."

"I will, Ms. Stiller."

"Tell her..." She drew in a deep breath, searching for the right words. There were none. ''Tell her I love her,'' she said at last. It fell far short of all that she needed to say, but that was all right. Her mother would understand.

The tears didn't start to flow until they were in the car.

* * *

Home. Thank God. Normalcy.

She drew in a deep breath on the porch while Steve opened the door. Letting go of all the tension, all the relief, everything she'd cried about on the long ride home. It was all right if Steve saw that—he'd married her for better or for worse—but she wouldn't bring it home to her children.

She felt different, somehow. No, that wasn't right. She felt as if she should be different, and she kept poking around inside her own consciousness to figure out where the difference was. Sharing a body with someone was the ultimate intimacy. Could you do that and not be changed by it? Could someone use your body and brain for a whole day and not leave her mark somewhere inside you, etched into one biochemical pathway or another?

Her friend Diane came running to the door as it opened, saw she was all right, and hugged her. "You're okay!"

"Of course I'm okay." She still had the tissue rose in her hand, and hugging Diane back without crushing it was no small feat. "The children—"

"Amy's in the kitchen. Mark and Simon are asleep. I thought you wouldn't want the little ones to wait up for you."

Two children in bed. Good. Soon she'd put Amy to bed herself, and that would be normal, too. Rhythms of life, reasserting themselves. She needed that right now.

She managed to wriggle out of her jacket without crushing the tissue flower. She could hear the dog barking from the backyard, begging to be let back in. Steve grinned as he hung up their coats and then went out to get him.

"No problems?" Marian asked, as they walked toward the kitchen. She wanted to hear it again. Wanted to savor the taste of the words.

"Nothing, really."

Was there an edge to her voice, a hint of uncertainty? Marian looked up sharply. "What? What is it? Did something happen?"

Diane hesitated. "She asked about it, Marian. They all did, but the boys gave up after I reassured them that you were okay. Amy...didn't. Children hear things, you know. They worry."

Marian felt a chill of dread seep into her heart. *She can't understand this. She's too young.* "What did you tell her?"

"That she'd have to wait for you to get home if she wanted more information. I knew how much you wanted to be the one to explain all this. She just...she wanted to know if a few things were true. Stories she'd heard from other children. Most of them weren't true, and they were pretty scary. She just needed reassurance." Diane bit her lip as she watched her for reaction. Somewhat nervously, Marian thought. "Just reassurance."

Marian forced herself to hold back all the sharp things she wanted to say. What good would it do now? She'd waited too long to choose the right words for Amy. Now someone else had done it for her. Berating Diane about it after the fact would get her nowhere.

You knew it had to happen someday. Time technology is part of her world; you can't hide it from her forever.

She found Amy at the kitchen table working on a jigsaw puzzle. It was one of Marian's own, a hard one. For a moment the girl didn't seem to notice her standing there in the doorway, but then the dog barked as it came bounding into the house, and Amy turned around. . .and her face broke into a broad grin of welcome as she saw Marian standing there. "Mom!"

"Hi, honeybee." She came up to the girl and tousled her curls. "I'm home now." Amy threw her arms around her with melodramatic glee, clearly delighted to have her home again. *See? Things are going to be all right. You were worried over nothing.* "I brought you a gift from Grandma." She knelt down so her eyes were on a level with the girl's, and held out the rose. "She used to make these when she was very young, before she got arthritis. See? It's all made out of tissues." Amy looked at the flower inquisitively and prodded it a few times, but didn't take it from her. "What are you doing, a puzzle?" Marian pulled up a chair to sit down. "That looks like a hard one."

"Diane said it was too hard for me. I told her I could do it if I wanted."

Marian laughed. "And so you can!" God, the laughter felt good. She saw her husband standing in the doorway and nodded to him. *Fine, everything's fine.* "You can do anything you want to." She scanned the pieces and saw one that had been sorted into the wrong pile. "Here, honey, try this one. See if you can tell me where it goes."

Amy didn't reach for the piece Marian offered, but picked up a blue one instead. "It's okay, Mom." The girl didn't look up at her. "I can do it myself."

Was there a note in her voice that was different than usual? *You're just being paranoid*, Marian told herself. *Everything's fine.* She watched her daughter for a few minutes more, studying the girl's face as she concentrated on the puzzle. Trying to see if there was some outward sign of…of whatever was wrong. Finally Marian picked up one of the pieces again, turning it thoughtfully in her fingers, and made her voice as calm as she could as she offered it to the girl. ''Look, here's a corner piece. Where do you suppose that goes?"

For a moment there was silence. Amy didn't reach for the piece that Marian held. She didn't do anything, for a moment. Then: "It's okay, Mom." Her voice was so quiet, so steady. "I don't need you to help me. Really."

Marian tried to speak, but her voice caught in her throat. The words of the counselor echoed in her head, not gentle words this time, but every sound a thorn. *Were your parents there for you, Ms. Stiller? Don't you owe them something for that?*

"I'm okay," Amy repeated, and she looked down again to work on the puzzle.

Marian watched her for a moment longer. Then she rose and left the room. The dog yapped at her ankles, but she ignored him. Steve started to ask what was wrong, but she waved him to silence. How could you explain the loss of something which never even had a name? How were you supposed to address fear in a child, when you couldn't make your own go away?

It wasn't until she got to her room and shut the door behind her that she realized she had crushed the tissue flower.

AUTHOR'S NOTE *for* DOWNTIME

I began writing this story many years ago, but it was a difficult subject to tackle, and when my mother's health starting going downhill, it hit too close to home; I had to put it away for a while. Mom spent her final years going in and out of the hospital, and I moved in with her for the last six months, to hold her hand while she was dying. In her last days, we talked about what she would do if she could have a reprieve from sickness, and just live like a normal person for a few days. Was there some experience she regretted passing up, a dream she longed to fulfill, that she would use the time for?

She told me that what she wanted most were the things we take for granted in our youth. To take a shower without assistance. To walk through a garden without gasping for breath. To eat all the foods she had been forbidden to taste for years. "If I knew I was going to die tomorrow," she told me, "I would eat a pastrami sandwich from Ben's."

I would have paid any price to be able to give her those things.

We buried her with a pastrami sandwich from Ben's, to accompany her to the afterlife. And years after her death, when the pain of losing her had subsided enough for me to write about the experience, I took up this story again. Because of the insight my mother gave me, I consider it my most meaningful work.

TRICK OR TREAT

Celebrate, young ones
Safe in the night
What is the past to you?
Costumes and makeup
Candy delight
Meaning enough for youth.

Once there were demons
Coursing the night
Drawn by the evening's fire.
Once there were spirits
Fragile and dim
Nameless in their desire.

Once there were deities
Summoned with song
Hungry and dark and cold.
Once there was chanting
Once there was blood
Gateways to places old.

Sing of them now, child
Call to the dead
Welcome them with your song.
Words are remembered
If meaning forgot
Power unnamed, but strong.

Paint your mask scarlet
Laugh at the fear
Dance in the pumpkin's glare.
Customs eternal
Sacrifice made
Call to them... if you dare.

AUTHOR'S NOTE *for* TRICK OR TREAT

In 1999 I was invited to write a book for White Wolf, part of their canon material for the role-playing game "Vampire: The Dark Ages." THE ERCIYES FRAGMENTS described the dark origins of the vampire race, written in a poetic style inspired by the biblical Psalms. While I was working on it, the same dark muse inspired me to write several other poems with supernatural themes. I've included a few of my favorites in this book.

An excerpt from FRAGMENTS appears later in the collection.

TERMS OF ENGAGEMENT

I made a deal with the roaches.

Mind you, it wasn't something I wanted to do. The way I'd been raised, bugs were something you talked to through the business end of a can of Raid, and the language consisted of one word: *Die!* My parents' home had been hermetically sealed by window and door experts, and any insect that mistook its climate-controlled confines for suitable territory was quickly—and terminally—taught the error of its ways. Houses were for humans, not insects.

Yes, I knew there were places where people didn't have the money or inclination to wage war so successfully against things that crept and slithered, the same way I knew there were striped horses in Africa and creatures in Australia that carried their young in a pouch. But those things weren't in my world, you understand. In my world, the closest you ever came to a cockroach was watching an insect documentary on PBS…and when the commercial came on you got up and washed your hands anyway, just because watching it made you feel so creepy.

Then I moved to Georgia.

I was in grad school then, and in grad school you didn't get to live in a hermetically sealed environment. You lived in a little apartment carved out of an aging house, that boasted of "great atmosphere" and "proximity to the college" rather than things like "living space" and "working appliances." The living room wall might have had a little hole cut into it, in which a tiny air conditioner was placed in deference to Yankee tastes (my southern friends all assured me that air conditioning was unhealthy), but the latter was mostly for cosmetic purposes, as it couldn't handle the kind of heat the Georgia sun belted out. Next door to the west would be a fraternity house, which meant an ancient mansion taken over by beer-swilling college boys with the personal hygiene habits of sewer rats and the social habits of....well, let's just say the cockroaches loved it there. To the east would be a sorority house, whose members valued the condition of their property a bit more than the guys did, and maintained it by partying on the street in front of your apartment instead of at their own place, leaving enough trash behind to feed a six-legged army.

At night the cockroaches would come out and dance on the sidewalk. I'm not kidding. You'd be walking down the street your first night in town, looking straight ahead like Yankees are taught to do (gotta watch for muggers!), grateful that the blazing sun had set at last, when suddenly, squish! You would look down, wondering what the hell you had stepped on...and you saw a few dozen roaches contemplating the same question. They were all over the sidewalk when night fell, celebrating the pleasures of cool concrete, or something like that, and you couldn't just ignore them or your shoes would be a mess, so you had to actually watch them, every step of the way, all the way home. Big ones and small ones, aggressive ones and shy ones...all dancing around as if they were in Times Square and the New Year's Eve ball had just dropped.

My friends assured me the big ones weren't really roaches, but some other kind of insect instead. That was supposed to make things better. I suppose when a creepy bug runs across your kitchen counter and it's three inches long (I am not exaggerating) and it looks like a roach and moves like a roach, it helps a lot to tell yourself, "Hey, it's only a palmetto bug, calm down!" I mean, maybe there are some people who find that kind of knowledge comforting, but in my book it's in the same category as "daddy long legs isn't really a spider."

Point is...You couldn't get away from them, no matter how hard you tried.

I had one of those little apartments, complete with the air

conditioner in a hole in the wall. The hole might have matched the air conditioner once, but years of vibrations and leaky drips had eaten away at the plaster surrounding, until, if you crouched in front of it just right, you could see the sunlight shining through on three sides of it. Highway for insects, to be sure. So I plastered that up, just like all the other grad students had done before me, but it didn't help much, because while you were closing up one hole there was another one being eaten away at the corner of a back window, or through the back of a closet, or somewhere else that cockroaches wanted to be.

It was war, plain and simple.

Trouble was, I was losing.

Oh, I'd started with all the best things an army could have: good spirit, excellent supplies, and a solid game plan. I had roach traps inside all my kitchen cabinets and cans of Raid within easy reach in every room, and after two months of particularly bad infestation I even got my landlord to bring in a professional exterminator. All of which just served to breed better roaches. Think about it. The ones who got caught in the traps were the stupid ones who couldn't tell *food* from *danger*, and you just took them out of the gene pool. The ones the exterminator got were the ones that couldn't run away fast enough, or maybe they were too territorial to know when a battle was lost and they needed to retreat and regroup in some other grad student's apartment. Ditto the gene pool exit for those guys. So the next generation, when it returned—and it would return—was less likely to get caught in traps, less likely to be at home when the exterminator called, and more likely to have cousins who came for a visit when the apartment next door was being sprayed.

If you're thinking 'you can't win'…you're right.

Did you know that roaches are one of the oldest forms of life on earth? And that if Georgia were hit with a nuclear bomb tomorrow, and the radiation was so hot that all the humans died, the roaches would get on just fine?

All of which does not comfort you when it's three in the morning and you wake up because something with six legs and antennae has decided your face is the place it wants to be.

I won't bore you with tales of all my many losing battles. They were the same battles that women have fought since the beginning of time, and I lost them for the same reasons my cave-dwelling ancestors probably lost them thousands of years ago. Whatever you do to roaches, they figure it out and learn how to work around you. And even if you manage to kill a bunch of them off, there are always more, ready to take their place.

One day I was at a friend's house. There were a lot of people over, mostly grad students griping about one class or another, and our host was doing something at the sink, when he let out a yelp suddenly and called us all over. We came running, but by then the thing he'd seen was gone.

"They've adapted!" he cried, and he told us breathlessly about a pair of roaches he'd seen, with translucent shells that matched the countertop. Yes, those creepy bastards had finally bred a variation that allowed them to match kitchen laminate, making them all but invisible in a modern urban environment! It was Darwinian evolution in action, and we were all pretty damn awed by it.

You know what was creepiest about that moment, in retrospect? That not one of us doubted it had happened! Not one of us doubted that roaches were indeed adaptable enough to evolve a slick change like that, and do it in time to cash in on current countertop fashions, before the trending colors changed and they were visible again. But in fact they hadn't done that, I found out later. It turns out that when roaches are first born they have naturally translucent shells for about a month, that darken later as they harden. But did we ask back then if that was possible? No. Did we harbor any doubt that the roaches had done what my friend claimed, and developed a new weapon in the eternal war for kitchen dominance? Of course not. Roaches might be our enemy, but they were a respected enemy, and we did not kid ourselves one iota about their capacity to innovate, genetically or otherwise.

That night I made a deal with the roaches in my apartment. That is, I offered them a deal. Since I'd spent the better part of two years killing them, they were understandably wary of sending anyone out to parley with me, but I went into the kitchen where I knew most of them were hiding, and I made them an offer loud enough for all to hear. I figured they'd let me know if it was acceptable or not.

"Look guys", I said, "I can't stand you being here, and you're obviously not going to leave no matter how many times I spray the place, so we've hit a bit of a stalemate. I'm betting you don't like this situation any more than I do. So I'm going to offer you a compromise. You can live in my apartment all you want, you can eat all the food you find that's out in the open, when the lights go off…but I don't want to see you. Does that sound fair?"

I listened for a minute, and there were no roaches telling me I was being unreasonable, so I went on. "Here's the deal, guys. Every room I go into, I'm gonna turn on the light first. No more of me wandering around in the dark; you'll all have fair warning that I'm coming. When you see that light, you go running for cover. And anyone who's out of sight by the time I arrive is safe. I won't set traps for them, I won't spray their homes, nothing. The rest…the rest are fair game."

It was a devious plan, and I'm not sure the roaches fully grasped its brilliance. You see, not only was I offering to spare those roaches whose behavior was suitably discrete, I'd be breeding their good habits into the swarm. By killing only those who stayed out when the lights were on, I'd be giving a reproductive advantage to those who instinctively ducked for cover right away. Eventually I'd have bred that quality into the local population as a whole, and voila! I'd never have to see another roach again.

Darwin was a genius, wasn't he?

"Oh," I added, as I left the kitchen (turning out the light as I did so), "stay out of the bedroom, would you?" I didn't offer a deal to cover that, but I thought they might be willing to throw it in, good faith gesture and all that.

I should note at this point that my boyfriend thought I was a raving loon. That isn't quite as judgmental as it sounds, since on a normal day he didn't think I was exactly a poster child for rational thinking. That's because he was a business major, and anything that could not be graphed out on a chart or recorded on a spreadsheet was, for him, not worth paying attention to. Since I was an artist, that included most of my life. So he spent most of his time with me trying not to express what he really thought about my profession, which was all right, because at least he tried. What more could you ask out of a poor business major? The sex was pretty good, at least. That made up for a lot.

But this was evidently too much for him. *"You made a deal with the roaches?"*

"It's an experiment in natural selection," I tried to explain. "You see, Darwinian theory—"

But he wasn't having any of it. He lectured me for half an hour on the craziness of trying to make deals with insects, which made me wonder if the sex was really that good. I mean, even an artist has her limits. He came one step short of saying I was crazy enough to be committed, but only just one step. Listening to him rage, I wondered what the roaches thought of it all, from their hiding places in the kitchen. God knows he was ranting loudly enough for every roach in the apartment complex to hear him.

Could I actually alter a species to suit my needs? Was the mere thought of doing so the ultimate in hubris, or a logical adaptation to our environmental rivalry? If the roaches in my apartment came to bear a genetic predisposition to "play by the rules", might they, in their romantic dalliances with neighboring roaches, pass the lesson on? My friends were fascinated by these and other questions, and demanded daily dispatches from me on how things were going in the War Zone. One even expressed regret that he had not studied my roach population before my experiment began, so that he could use the results as part of his master's thesis.

And the news was…it was working. Sure, it was weird for me at first, reaching into the bathroom to flick on the light a full minute before I looked inside. And sure, it was messy at first, with all the roaches that hadn't gotten with the program needing to be dispatched before anything else was done. Sometimes in the middle of the night you just want to do your business and go back to bed, you know? But damn it all if after a few weeks there weren't few and fewer roaches to kill. I knew I hadn't gotten them all, so it had to be that the rest were learning the house rules. Maybe they would teach their young, and help the Darwinian thing along.

But the better my experiment went, the more upset my boyfriend seemed to get about it. "You're obsessed with the damn roaches!" he accused, in a tone of voice that made it clear the real crime was that I was not obsessed enough with him. "Do you really think they give a damn about this 'treaty' you have with them?" He even got mad at me for leaving the bathroom light on when he was sleeping at my place. But I knew he wouldn't respect my deal with the roaches enough to turn it on in himself, and I didn't want any of my well-trained little roommates to be trapped in the spotlight when they hadn't had fair warning. How could I expect all their people to respect our deal if my people didn't?

One night we had a really big fight. I'd gone a month without seeing a single roach anywhere, and, well, it was a big deal. People who love you are supposed to share in your triumphs, right? Or at least pretend they do? But he just got angrier than ever, and went off on a tirade about how anyone whose life revolved around the learning curve of roaches (he said it that way, "learning curve", as if it was some business thing he'd charted out) maybe didn't belong in his life. So I yelled back, and then I cried, and he finally stopped yelling at me but he didn't cry, and finally we made up. Sorta. We had sex, anyway. But there's only so many times sex can fix a broken relationship, and somewhere in the middle of it I felt like we'd just passed that point.

It was an oppressively hot night, and the little air conditioner in the living room wall was pretty far from my bedroom. In the summertime cool air only gets so far before the Georgia humidity beats it to death. I tossed and turned and finally I guess I woke him up, because he whispered to me, "You okay, babe? You need anything?" You could tell from his tone of voice he felt a little guilty about the fight we'd had, which was fine by me.

"Just hot," I said. It would have been a lot cooler without someone else in the bed, but that wasn't the kind of thing you said out loud. "Could you get me a glass of water, maybe?"

He nodded and got up to do it. I heard him pad his way to the kitchen in the darkness. For a brief moment I thought I should remind him about the lights, and then I thought, screw him. He didn't respect my deal with the roaches, so let him trip over a few in the dark. Maybe then he'd appreciate what I had accomplished and respect the rules of the house.

The bed was a lot cooler without him in it. I found a spot in the middle without any body heat at all and snuggled into it. In the distance I heard the fridge door open and the ice tray crackling as he broke the cubes apart. Ice. Good thought. I could almost forgive him, for bringing me ice. Then there was a loud thump, which at first I thought was the fridge door closing, but it really wasn't like that at all. Then silence.

"Hey!" No answer. I called his name. Still no answer. There was an odd scraping sound then, and the tinkling sound of ice cubes hitting each other. So he was still moving around in there, anyway. "You okay?" It really was dark. I shouldn't have let him feel his way in there without some kind of light.

He knew where the light switch was. He'd wanted to prove a point.

Finally he had just been gone too long for comfort. I got up from bed myself and went to the doorway, slid my hand around the doorjamb and flicked on the hall light. Counted to ten. Then I walked down the empty hall to my kitchen. It was quiet now, but I could see even from around the corner that he'd left the fridge door open. I slid my hand around the corner and turned on that light, then counted to ten. Then entered.

All quiet.

No boyfriend.

There were ice cubes on the floor. They were already starting to melt. Some of the water had been dragged in little trails across the linoleum, to a place right under the sink. The cabinet door there was partly open, as though someone had been getting something out of it, but then got interrupted.

Or putting something in.

For a few minutes I just stared at it, and then I walked very slowly to the half-open cabinet. I didn't store anything in there, as a rule, so there wasn't any reason to look inside. No reason at all. I contemplated the open door for a moment and then reached out and shut it. It was easy for a person to do. Would have been harder for bugs to manage…especially if their little hands were already being used for another task.

I guess maybe I could have done something else instead. Screamed my head off, or called in the exterminators, or turned on all the lights in the house and then transferred to some other college far, far away, where I never had to look at a Georgia cockroach again. Something like that. But I had told them they could have any food they found, when the lights were off. And they were staying out of the bedroom, just like I'd asked them to.

The bed had cooled off a bit by the time I got back to it, which was something, anyway. I lay in bed for a while listening to the soothing silence, and then slowly drifted off to sleep.

It's easier to sleep alone in the summer.

AUTHOR'S NOTE *for* TERMS OF ENGAGEMENT

The part about the roaches is true.

While attending grad school in Georgia, I lived in a small, rundown apartment, complete with roaches. Unable to get rid of them because my neighbors would just offer them sanctuary until it was safe for the bugs to come back, I decided to try an experiment, and see if I could train my roaches to keep out of sight, so at least I would not have to look at them. It worked exactly as described here, albeit without complicated treaty negotiations.

At the same time, unbeknownst to me, my brother was facing the same problem in his apartment up north, and also decided to experiment with behavior modification. He told his roaches they could have free use of one room of his house, provided they did not go anywhere else. He killed all the ones he saw elsewhere, but not in that room, and eventually his local population did indeed get the message. The problem with his plan, though, was that he had to use food to tempt them into that room to begin with, which resulted in a mild population increase. Okay, maybe not so mild.

It was not until many years later that we compared notes, and realized we had been running similar roach experiments at the same time. Great minds think alike, I guess.

The boyfriend in this story is wholly fictional. My real boyfriend was wholly supportive of me, and one of the sweetest guys I have ever met. I would never have fed him to roaches.

SOUL MATE

All things considered, the arts and crafts festival was not as bad as it could have been.

There was a lot of high-end jewelry being sold, polished gold and silver sculpted into interesting shapes, and several booths featured the paintings of prominent abstract artists. The latter was a happy surprise for Josie. A show like this usually had stall after stall of representational paintings, passionless renderings of trees and farmhouses and ducks (there always seemed to be ducks) just waiting to be hung on the wall behind an ugly flowered couch. And of course there were always crowds of sunburned tourists standing around each painting, chattering about how wonderful the ruddy hue of that aging barn was, or how a particular beam of sunlight, trickling through the branches of a willow tree, was just the *right* tone of amber. At such times she was acutely aware of the limits of her own vision, and the fact that she could not perceive the same subtle distinctions of color that other people could. Abstract art, by contrast, was a purely private indulgence. It either spoke or you or it didn't. No one else told you what it was supposed to look like, or felt that there was something wrong with you if you could not share their perspective.

She wandered around for nearly an hour before the day's heat finally got to her, then made her way back to the far end of the festival grounds, where her friend Karen had set up her wares. The U-shaped table was located next to an enormous oak tree, whose branches had offered a modicum of shade during the first part of the day. But the sun had since shifted westward, moving the shade away from the display, and the beach umbrella set up to compensate wasn't big enough to shelter the whole table. Racks of crystal earrings caught on fire as the sunlight hit them, blazing with palpable heat. Did that intensify the colors in the glass, or bleach them out? The only hue that stood out to Josie was a brilliant cobalt at the end of the rack. But that was hardly a surprise. Subtle color combinations were lost on her.

"How is business?" Josie asked, settling into a small plastic chair by the side of the table.

"Like you'd expect." Karen reached back into a cooler behind her, pulled out an ice-cold soda, and handed it over. Josie held it against her face for a moment before breaking it open, letting her skin absorb its wonderful chill. "People don't spend as much money in this kind of heat." She sipped from her own soda. "Everything will wind down soon, I expect. The stained glass people have already left. How did your shopping go?"

"There was some nice jewelry. Nothing I desperately need to own. Except for Romero's stuff, which I can't afford." She sighed. "He's got a lotus blossom necklace to die for—art noveau design, with freshwater pearls in the blossoms—but…well, you know his prices. A real work of art, though."

"You always did like that Art Noveau stuff."

She nodded and took a deep drink from her can, shutting her eyes to savor the flow of effervescent liquid down her throat. In the midst of the day's heat, it was almost as good as diving into a waterfall.

"Hey." Karen nudged her with an elbow. "Speaking of works of art."

Opening her eyes once more, Josie followed her friend's gaze across the festival grounds. There was a dirt road dividing Karen's row of tables from the next one, where a number of couch-painting vendors had hung their indistinguishable wares. At the end of the line was a small display of more interesting work, including a few Vernon Miller prints. Bright, bold, and clean of line, they were as refreshing to her soul as the cold soda had been to her body, and for a moment she forgot her purpose and just admired them. But Karen's elbow in her ribs urged her back to the business at hand, and so she scanned the whole of the stall, wondering what it was that her friend wanted her to look at.

"Oh..."

He was standing opposite one of the larger prints, a Miller lithograph that Josie had been admiring earlier in the day. His attention was wholly focused upon the work, as if the rest of the world had ceased to exist. The sense of aesthetic communion was so intense it seemed almost sexual, and Josie found herself being drawn to both him and the lithograph. Or maybe that had nothing to do with his concentration. Maybe the sight of a man that attractive admiring her favorite artist was a pleasurable thing in its own right. Only the side of his face was visible, but it was finely sculpted, perfectly proportioned. He had sun-bronzed skin and strong shoulders, and an aura of self-confidence bordering on arrogance which many women found sexy. His white linen shirt was perfectly pressed, his dark hair perfectly coifed, his leather shoes perfectly polished. He was the kind of man who looked as good as he did because he invested time and effort into doing so. The kind of man you admired in magazines, but did not expect to meet in person.

"Ten bucks says he's gay", Karen whispered.

"You think?"

Karen chuckled. "You know the rules. The pretty ones are always gay, married, or living in their mother's basement."

The stranger turned in their direction, as if something on their side of the road had drawn his attention. Josie caught a flash of deep brown eyes as he scanned the fairgrounds, a hint of some exotic heritage in their depths. Not a type she normally dated, but damn, he was nice to look at.

"Or serial killers," she whispered back, completing the formula.

And then, unexpectedly, he looked directly at them, and met Josie's gaze. His eyes fixed on her with disconcerting intensity, and she felt herself shiver.

He left the Miller stall and started towards them.

"Holy shit," Karen whispered, and she started straightening the necklaces in her display for cover. Josie lifted up a hand to smooth stray wisps of her blond hair back into place. It was a hopeless task. A long day of sun and sweat had made her feel like a drowned rat; she couldn't have looked worse for meeting a man like this, she thought, if she'd dressed for the occasion.

And then he was right there in front of her, all tan and gym-toned and looking like he just stepped out of a fashion spread. "I saw you admiring the lithographs."

From somewhere she found her voice. "I like Miller's work a lot."

He smiled. "Then we have that much in common." He glanced down at the table, and reached out to stroke a pair of crystal earrings. He wore no wedding ring, Josie noted, nor was there any tan line to imply he should be wearing one. Not married, then. *One down, three to go.* "Good art speaks to the soul, don't you think?"

"So does bad art." She smiled. "It just says things we may not want to hear."

"Perhaps." His smile was winning. His teeth were perfect. The kind of perfection that didn't come naturally, but had to be paid for, tooth by tooth. "Is this yours?" He indicated the jewelry.

She shook her head, nodding towards Karen, who offered, "Mine. All handmade, sterling silver, and the crystal is Swarovski." With a mischievous gleam in her eye she added, "Perhaps there's something here your girlfriend would like?"

A faint smile flickered across his lips as he looked at her; he knew the bait for what it was. "I have no girlfriend."

"A boyfriend, then?" Karen smiled sweetly.

Josie found that she was holding her breath. But he only chuckled and turned back to her. "Forgive me," he said. "I'm being rude. Stephan Mayeaux." He offered his hand.

"Josephine Ballard. Josie, usually. And this is Karen Foster."

He held her hand for a moment longer than he had to; the contact made her skin tingle. For a moment—just a moment—it seemed there was a connection between them, something that mere physical touch could not explain. He nodded to Karen, polite but distant. Clearly it was Josie he was interested in. Or was that just wishful thinking on her part? Jesus, she was thinking like the heroine of a cheap romance novel. (Not that she ever read any of those, of course.)

Suddenly the strains of a rippling piano arpeggio dispelled her reverie; it took her a few seconds to recognize the melody as a Bach prelude. He pulled a cell phone out of his pocket, looked at the caller ID, and sighed. "I'm sorry. Please excuse me. I need to answer this."

He walked down the road a few steps and turned away from them. Josie could sense Karen trying to get her attention, but she didn't make eye contact with her. She was trying not to think about whether this man was really flirting with her, and what it might mean if he was.

He's not your type, you know that. Too self-focused. Too meticulous. Probably obsessive-compulsive. How do you make love to a man, if his biggest concern is that his hair might get mussed? He probably lives in the kind of house where nothing is ever out of place. Not a run-down Victorian, stuffed to the rafters with a lifetime of mementos, all in glorious disorder. What would he think of my place if he saw it?

It was a bad match. Really bad. That much was clear.

He slipped the phone back into his pocket as he returned to the table. "I'm sorry. There's trouble with an upcoming shipment. I'm going to have to go back to the gallery and deal with it."

"The gallery?"

"Northpoint gallery. On the lakefront. Mostly I carry things for the tourist trade, but you know…there's a new Miller coming in that I think you might like."

The words came out before she could stop them. "Is that an invitation?"

The dark eyes were fixed on her. Their intensity was unnerving. "If I had your phone number it might be."

Jesus. Jesus. She couldn't date an art dealer. What would happen when he realized she couldn't see half the things in his world? What would they talk about?

Something small and white nudged her arm. She looked down at the table and saw that Karen was offering her a business card, blank side up, along with a pen. After a moment's hesitation she took both, and wrote out her number as if in a daze. *Bad idea*, an inner voice cautioned. "Here," she said, giving the card to him. Wondering if her smile had ever looked as perfect as his. Maybe she should look into having her teeth whitened.

"I'll call you" he promised. And he nodded a polite farewell to them both before heading back down the road, toward the fairground exit.

The two friends looked at each other. For a moment they both said nothing.

Then Karen grinned. "Just make sure you check out his mother's basement before you sleep with him, will you?'

* * *

A woman.

He sits in the quiet darkness of his sleek and spotless apartment, moonlight washing over him, and thinks: I have chosen a woman.

He isn't quite sure why that happened. He certainly didn't plan it. But instinct, as always, is a powerful master. The moment he felt this one's scrutiny touch him—the moment she had connected to Miller's lithograph, and through that to him—he wanted her. Even before he had seen her face, or learned her name. it was not a desire born of intellect but of instinct, that burning fire deep within his soul which had been banked for far too long. Now the flames are rising up again, and they threaten to consume him whole if he does not feed them what they need.

A woman.

He's known for some time now that a change is imminent. He is familiar enough with the soul-deep restlessness that precedes such an event to know it for what it is, and has already been wondering where it will lead him. Will the next phase of his life be a comfortable and familiar thing, ushered in without effort or hardship? Or does he hunger for something more challenging this time, an experience that will set his senses alight with fear, so that his new life will be birthed in a pool of adrenalin-charged uncertainty? His last few lovers were all men, so similar in body and mindset that they were all but interchangeable. True, he savored the subtle differences between them as with a fine wine, reveling in delicate distinctions of taste that only a true connoisseur could detect, while taking perverse pleasure in the fact that no one on the outside could ever share his perceptions. But moving from one to another has been as effortless as crossing the street: a sonata of adaptation. One of them liked silk shirts. Another preferred linen. Variations on a theme.

This one will be different. Jazz. Cacophony.

A woman.

He has not taken on a challenge like this in a very long time. Several lifetimes, in fact.

Perhaps he is overdue.

Midnight shimmers across the polished floorboards as he picks up his phone, draws out her card, and starts to dial the number on it.

* * *

Josie had never been so nervous about a date in her life. Or spent so long preparing for one. It took her hours just to find the right outfit to wear—not her usual bohemian garb, with layers of embroidered gauze, but a neater, simpler style, that would hopefully appeal to his meticulous taste—and then hours more to clean up the house to the point where, if he wound up coming inside, he would not be scared off. Not that the place was messy, exactly, but her penchant for hanging onto mementos from all the high points of her life did make for a cluttered house, and he didn't strike her as the kind of man who appreciated clutter as an art form.

This is crazy, she thought. *We probably have nothing in common. Surely he'll figure that out within an hour, and the whole relationship will be over before dessert.*

But then he showed up at her door and all those doubts vanished. Not because she'd necessarily been wrong about him…simply because she didn't care.

He was dressed in a softer mode tonight. Maybe he had sensed that his former appearance was intimidating to her. There were even one or two hairs out of place, as if the wind had disturbed them. Was that genuine disarray, or artful affectation? She didn't know him well enough to say for sure, but it soothed her nerves to think it might be the former. It made him seem…well, more human.

They would find common ground, she told herself. She would make it happen.

But surprisingly little effort was needed in that regard. He took her to a seafood restaurant on the eastern shore of the lake, without even knowing it was one of her favorites. She let him pick out the wine for them, and he chose the same Riesling she would have ordered for herself. He even chose one of her favorite dishes for his own meal, though she'd never said a word about liking it.

It was heartening, but it was also eerie. For a brief moment Karen's warning echoed in her brain, and she wondered if he might not have gained all that knowledge from watching her eat on some former occasion. Would she know what a stalker looked like, if she met one? But then the conversation turned to other things, things he could not possibly have known about her from simple observation. Passages from literature that touched her spirit. Musical compositions that made her soul sing with joy, or weep with sorrow. As he shared a glimpse of his own special, secret moments, she was struck by how alike they were, deep inside. As if they were twins who had been separated long ago, now rediscovering each other.

Except for the matter of art.

She didn't have the courage to tell him about her limited color vision, or how it affected her perception of the visual arts. Didn't have the heart to explain to him that her familiarity with Jordan Miller's work had more to do with keeping Karen company at art festivals than any great appreciation of the lithographic medium. That didn't mean she wasn't a creative soul at heart, but her own personal medium was the author's pen. Writing was an art form she could understand, and the subtle gradations of a finely crafted poem were as real to her, and as beautiful, as any brushstroke by Picasso was to him.

He'll invite me to see his gallery, she thought. There was a cold fluttering in the pit of her stomach at the thought that their strange compatibility, so fragile and new, might not survive the test of such a visit.

But for now, it was enough to eat dessert at an outdoor table overlooking the water, watching the sunset ripple across the waves. Stephan spoke in poetic terms about the color of the light, which was not the most comfortable moment for her, but the breeze tousled his hair while he spoke, and she focused on that. Sometimes she felt as if the man she was with tonight and the one she had met at the festival were two different people. Or perhaps the first one had become magically transformed, into her perfect suitor.

Really, she thought, *I should start writing romance novels.*

When the meal was over they walked along the beach together, and he kicked off his shoes to feel the wet sand squish between his toes, which was one of her own secret pleasures. They laughed and they talked and maybe they had a little too much wine, because they started running down the beach together, splashing through the water like children. How strange it all was, and how wonderful! As if she had known him all her life. As if they had a thousand memories in common, rather than only a few precious hours.

And in the end she discovered that he did not really mind rumpled clothes, or getting sand in his hair, half as much as she'd expected. Which was a good thing, because neither did she.

* * *

"So what do you think?"

The Northpoint Gallery was a sleek modern construct, whose architecture seemed better suited to midtown Manhattan than an upstate resort town. The darkness of early evening only intensified that effect, glass and steel reflecting fractured images from the more traditional buildings surrounding it, producing a ghostly mosaic.

It was exactly the kind of place she would have expected him to own, back when she'd first met him, but it seemed a strange mismatch to the man she was dating now. She blinked as she entered, trying to reconcile the two identities.

Inside was a gallery as sleekly modern as the façade, with abstract paintings hung on stark white walls and strange modern sculptures poised atop pedestals of burnished steel. It resonated money and taste in cold, carefully controlled doses. The kind of thing she had happily left behind when she'd moved out of the city years ago.

"Tourists from the city shop here when the rustic surroundings start to get to them," he explained. "There are only so many candle shops you can visit before you go mad."

She smiled slightly, trying to feel comfortable in this alien environment. "So you cater to their madness?"

"It's proven to be a lucrative market. Would you like some coffee?"

Before she could answer, a young Hispanic-looking man emerged from behind one of the angled walls. He was dressed in a silk shirt and expensive designer slacks, and was as meticulously well-groomed as Stephen had been back at the fairgrounds. No doubt they shopped at the same boutique, and probably used the same hair gel.

The newcomer raised an eyebrow as he looked at Stephan, then at her, then back to Stephan: the message of incredulity was clear. *You're with a woman?*

"Josephine, this is Pietro, my assistant." Stephan nodded towards him. "Pietro, would you please bring the lady some coffee?"

"Black with sugar," she offered.

Pietro moved off wordlessly to obey. He had the same air she'd originally noted in Stephan, the natural arrogance of an urban sophisticate. But Stephan no longer had that air about him. Could a man change so much in just a few weeks? Or was she just seeing him differently, now that she knew him better?

Stephan led her around and showed her the artwork. They started with a collection of bronze sculptures that Josie could honestly appreciate. He knew the artist personally, and had interesting stories to tell about each piece. By the time he turned his attention to one of the larger paintings, she had a cup of coffee in her hand that she could play with to mask her nervousness.

But instead of talking about the painting, he just stared at it for a moment, as if something was not quite right. "That's odd," he murmured

"What is?"

He looked back at one of the statues and squinted, as if something about it puzzled him. Then back at the painting. "The lighting. It's not right." He called out to the back of the store, "Pietro!" When the assistant appeared he asked him, "Have we changed any of our bulbs recently?"

"Not that I'm aware of."

His brow furrowed as he looked back at the painting. "How strange…"

"Light bulbs?" Josie asked.

He nodded. "Ours are spectrum-balanced to be as close to neutral white as possible. So that all the colors will read true." He looked back at the painting. "Maybe it's an electrical issue. Color temperature drops when bulbs aren't operating at full capacity. I'll have an electrician check it out in the morning." He turned to her, a warm smile on his lips. "I'll have to bring you back here when you can see everything in the proper light."

The thought that he might be sensitive enough to color that changing a light bulb would matter was almost enough to make her laugh out loud, but she managed to stifle the impulse. "I'd like that," she said solemnly."

"Meanwhile…I have a gift for you."

He took a small, flat box out of his breast pocket and handed it to her. Curious, she opened it. Inside was a vintage gold-and-pearl pendant, flowers with pearls in the blossoms. Art Nouveau.

"Happy two week anniversary," he told her.

"It's beautiful," she whispered. "I love this style. How did you know?"

He chuckled softly. "We have so much else in common, I took a chance we shared a taste in jewelry as well. Here, let me help you."

He positioned the pendant in the hollow of her throat, then reached around to the back of her neck to work the clasp. As he did so she caught sight of Pietro out of the corner of her eye, dark eyes glowering, mouth pursed in obvious disapproval. Was it jealousy? Had they been lovers in the past, perhaps? That might explain his expression.

Yes, she thought to him, *that's right, Stephan is dating a blond, blue-eyed, nature-loving antique junkie now, who wears peasant shirts and Dr. Scholl's sandals. And, by the way, she's a woman. So deal with it, pretty boy!*

* * *

It was Karen who suggested a double date. It had been weeks since the two of them had seen each other, she said, and since Josie and her new beau seemed to be inseparable now, it seemed the easiest way to get together.

She sounded bitter about the situation, but that was only to be expected. The two of them had been sisters in all but name for as far back as Josie could remember. This was the first time they'd been apart for so long. And to be fair, Josie really had been neglecting her friends lately. Not by any grand design, of course. But there simply was a finite amount of time in her life, and Stephan Mayeaux was now taking up most of it.

She couldn't wait for Karen to see how well they were suited to one another. Surely that chemistry would be evident, even over dinner. Not until now had she realized how much she wanted her best friend to approve of this man. Not until that happened could this relationship be considered truly perfect.

Karen suggested they meet at an Italian restaurant, a quiet and friendly pace where they could all chat comfortably. Her own date was a shy sort who didn't add much to the conversation, but Stephan was nothing short of charming. His business with the gallery had given him enough experience with art shows that he was soon sharing anecdotes with Karen as if they were old friends, and Josie was flushed with happiness. When Karen excused herself from the table after the main course she did the same, anxious for a moment alone with her friend to hear what she thought.

Karen said nothing to her on the way to the ladies' room. When she entered, she walked down the row of stalls, checking to see if they were occupied.

"Well?" Josie asked impatiently. "What do you think?"

After confirming that all the stalls were empty, Karen hesitated. "I think there's something not right about him, Josie. I'm sorry."

Josie was stunned. "I don't understand."

"Do you not see what he's doing? Or do you just not care?"

A cold shiver ran down Josie's spine. "See what?"

"That he's copying your mannerisms. Your expressions. Even the cadence of his voice is like yours now." She shook her head. "I met him when you did, Josie. Remember? I know what he was like before he started dating you. And I tell you, he's copying your body language now. Maybe just unconsciously, I don't know. But that's still pretty weird, don't you think?"

Josie blinked. The accusation was…well, it was so bizarre that she could hardly absorb it. Finally she managed to force out, "I'm sure you're imagining things."

"You've got this little thing you do with your spoon when you eat soup, do you know that? You run it around the rim of the bowl just before you start eating. Just a little unconscious thing, I'm sure; I've watched you do it for years. And tonight…he did it too. That's very strange, Josie." Her eyes narrowed. "No. It's more than strange. It's downright creepy."

"You think he's mocking me?"

"No. No. I don't think it's that at all. It's just that…how much do you know about him? I mean, *really* know about him?"

"I know that we have great chemistry," she said defensively. "And couples with great chemistry sometimes come to resemble one another. Sometimes they even have mannerisms in common, just like you're describing."

"Yes—after ten years of marriage, not three weeks of dating." She paused, "You know, I hate to bring this up, but there's a kind of mental illness where a man will adopt the personality of other people…"

"You watch too much TV," she snapped.

"That doesn't mean I'm wrong," Karen pointed out.

Josie turned away; she didn't want her friend to see the tears that were coming to her eyes. After a moment Karen reached out and put a hand on her shoulder. "Josie, I love you. You know that. I wouldn't do anything to hurt you, ever. But this guy…something about him is just not right. Please trust me on this one."

"You think I should break up with him?"

The hand fell away. She heard Karen sigh. "I think that's your choice to make. But I would, if I were you. In a heartbeat."

Josie left the rest room.

There was a short hallway right outside the door. She leaned against the wall there, her shoulders trembling, and tried to pull herself together. She couldn't let Stephan see her like this. He wouldn't understand.

Karen's hurt, she thought, *and she's jealous. We've been inseparable for so long, and suddenly someone has come between us. Of course she's going to see the worst in him. Of course she's going to hope I will end it.*

It wasn't a perfect explanation, she knew. It probably wouldn't stand up to close inspection later. But it was something she could cling to right now, to get through the rest of the meal without tears, and that was what mattered most.

* * *

"You okay?" Stephan asked her.

She huddled down into the passenger seat of his car, resting her cheek against the sleek black Italian leather. "I'm okay," she said quietly.

"You were pretty quiet after you came back to the table."

"I had a lot to think about it."

He was driving with one hand through the steering wheel, his wrist resting on the central hub. It was a position that would block the airbag if there were an accident. Josie's mother was always on her case about her doing the same thing.

I'm falling in love with you, she thought miserably. *I don't want there to be anything wrong with you.*

"Something your friend Karen said?"

All the rest of the meal, she had watched him closely. Listening to him closely. Trying to decide if Karen was right. Wanting with all her heart to believe her friend was wrong. "She thought we were moving too fast." It was better to give him some kind of explanation than try to deny that anything had happened. "She just wanted me to be careful, that's all."

"Careful?" There was an edge to his voice now; clearly he didn't like the fact that Karen was interfering in their relationship. "Careful about what?"

She shrugged.

"If there's a problem, we can talk about it. You know that there's nothing we can't handle, if we face it together."

A lump rose in her throat. "I know," she whispered.

He looked back at the road. They were approaching a major intersection, and the light had changed while they were talking.

He didn't stop.

Cars screeched to a halt as they skidded out of the way, trying to avoid a collision. Stephan turned his wheel wildly, trying to avoid a truck that was suddenly in his path. Time seemed to slow down as Josie grabbed the edges of her seat, her heart pounding so hard she thought it would burst from her chest. Everything seemed to be in slow motion. Cars screeched past her window at a surreal pace, giving her time to work out just how badly she would be crushed if they didn't turn aside in time.

And then, as quickly as it had begun, it was over. Stephan managed to pull over to the curb without hitting anyone, while the other cars began to sort themselves out and move past him. No one had been hurt, thank God, but Josie was badly shaken. So was Stephan, apparently; his hands were gripping the wheel so tightly that his knuckles were white.

For a moment they both just stared out the window, unable to speak. Then he reached down and put the car in park, and turned to face her. The look in his eyes was terrible, but it was not fear she saw there. It was anger.

"You're *colorblind.*" he accused.

"What the hell business is it of yours?" She was angry herself now, that he would follow up such a nerve-wracking experience with this accusation. Here she was still shaking after a near brush with death, and he was yelling at her about some piddling handicap that she hadn't confessed to him. "What difference does it make, anyway? It's my problem, not yours."

For a moment she thought that he was going to hit her. He looked that angry. Then, with a muttered curse, he fumbled his seat belt open, thrust open his door, and exited the car. When he was clear of the door he slammed it shut behind him, so hard that the whole vehicle shook.

She sat there in shock for a moment, then climbed out of the car herself. He was already halfway down the block, walking away at a swift clip.

"Stephan!"

He turned back to look at her. Her expression was so terrible that it made her take a step backwards. Rage. Pure rage.

At her? Over what?

Then he turned his back to her again and continued down the street. And it was all she could do to stand there, trembling, and try to catch her breath.

What the hell was that about?

* * *

GALLERY VANDALIZED

Northpoint Gallery was vandalized last night, sometime between 10 and 11 PM. Locals heard suspicious noises coming from inside the building and called in an alarm, but by the time police arrived, over $100,000 of original artwork had been destroyed, with extensive damage to the interior of the building as well.

Sheriff Leon Marshall is heading Northpoint's investigation into the case. While few details are being released to the public, the scope of the damage has prompted speculation that the vandalism might have been an act of rage directed at the owner, Mr. Stephan Mayeaux.

Mr. Mayeaux has thus far declined to comment upon the matter.

* * *

"Karen. Are you there? Please pick up if you are."

Silence.

"Karen, please call me as soon as you get in. Please. I need to talk to you."

Silence on the line. Faint static in the distance. Nothing else.

Her heart cold with misgiving, Josie finally hung up. God alone knew what Karen would think when she got home and checked her messages. Josie had left at least half a dozen, and that was not counting all the times she had called and said nothing. But surely it wasn't unreasonable for her to be concerned. Karen was the kind of person who was joined at the hip to her cell phone, and the only way she'd be out of reach this long was if sunspots had wiped out all reception on earth.

So something was wrong.

Josie paced back and forth across the kitchen, trying to burn off some of her nervous energy. Stephan hadn't talked to her since that night in the car. And now there was news that his beloved gallery had been vandalized, and all his precious artwork destroyed, within an hour of their fight. Every time she tried to figure out what could possibly have happened, a cold knot formed in the pit of her stomach. Karen could have helped her sort it all out, but Karen was missing. Josie's whole world was upside down.

She hadn't tried to call Stephan yet. She kept picking up the phone to do so, and once she even started to dial his number, but she stopped before the connection could be made. She didn't know what to say to him. She needed for him to call her first, to tell her that everything was all right. Or at least to say something that would allow her to believe he hadn't destroyed the gallery himself.

What the hell had happened in the car?

No matter how many times she went over the incident in her mind, it made no sense to her. They'd been driving along, had a near-accident, and suddenly he had gotten angry at her for being colorblind. No; suddenly he had *realized* she was colorblind. That was the really weird part of it. The more she reviewed the scene in her mind, the more she became convinced that had been his actual moment of revelation. Knowledge had come to him in the wake of the accident, seemingly out of nowhere. Then he had turned on her.

It just made no sense.

She ached for him, as she had never ached for anyone before. Having him missing from her life was like having part of her soul excised: a spiritual amputation. But what would she say to him, if he did decide to call? Even if she were desperate enough to beg for forgiveness, or willing to grovel to bring him back…what exactly would she be groveling about?

With a sigh she got up and began to change the coffee filter, preparing to make another pot. She'd switched to decaf hours ago; her nerves couldn't handle anything stronger. Her left pinky finger was twitching, which was something it did when she was stressed to the breaking point. A warning sign.

And then the doorbell rang.

For a moment she froze. Then, hands shaking, she dropped the used filter into the trash can and hurried to the front hallway. She drew in a deep breath before opening the door.

It was Stephan.

He said nothing to her. Just waited. After a moment she backed away to give him room to come in. His anger seemed to have subsided, but there was a strange look in his eyes, that warned her to keep her distance. Was it possible he was dangerous? She didn't want to believe he would hurt her, but after that scene in the car anything was possible.

There is something not right about him, Karen had warned her.

But he only walked quietly into the living room, and she followed, equally silent. For a moment he just stood there, as if gathering his thoughts. She waited.

"I'm sorry," he said at last.

The knot in her gut loosened a tiny bit. She felt tears coming to her eyes, and struggled to fight them back.

"I'm sorry things are moving so fast," he continued. "Usually the process is much more…leisurely."

The dark brown eyes met hers. She could see herself reflected in them. Tiny mirrors.

"Your life and mine are not compatible," he told her. "I can't handle both of them at once. And I can't go back. I've tried that before, and it doesn't work."

He stepped forward, close to her, and put his hands on the sides of her face, cupping her cheeks gently. She trembled. Leaning over, he kissed her softly on the forehead. "I'm sorry," he whispered.

His left pinky twitched against her cheek.

A sudden wave of panic came over her. She tried to pull away from him, but it was hard to move. She felt as if they were attached, and she could not separate from him without tearing her own flesh to pieces.

"What are you?" she whispered. She struggled to calculate the distance she'd have to go to get to the front door, the alarm pad, the knife rack in the kitchen. Which was closest? "What do you want?"

He didn't answer. His eyes were dark and cold, without a hint of kindness in them.

Somehow she managed to jerk away from him, and tried to run to the door. But her feet felt as if hundred-pound weights were attached to them, and she only managed a few steps before she stumbled and fell. He knelt by her side and took her face in his hands again, and she could not break free of his grasp.

And then she looked up at him, and saw what he had become.

And screamed.

"It should have been gentler," her lover said quietly. "I should have taken you in your sleep. Nestled you in my arms. That's how it usually goes."

Visions began to race through Josie's mind. Memories from her youth. From adulthood. From yesterday. In the wake of each one there was a spark of pain, and then the memory was gone. Completely gone. As though it had never existed in the first place.

"You should have told me you were imperfect," the creature that had once been Stephan admonished her. "I never would have chosen you, had I known."

The memory of Karen flickered through her mind, and then vanished. Her last memory. Tears ran down her face, but she no longer remembered why she was crying.

The last thing she saw, before darkness claimed her, was her own face gazing down at her.

* * *

Peace.

The life he has lived for so long is gone, and with it all the hungers and passions that attended it. He can no longer see color properly—that is the unfortunate cost of this transition—but now that he has changed, he no longer has the same driving need to see color. That was a feature of Stephan, and Stephan is dead now. Josie takes pleasure in language, and now, finally, he has the capacity to understand that gift. How beautiful a simple phrase can be, when perfectly crafted! How thrilling, the discovery of a new and expressive word!

New memories are flooding his brain, reshaping neural pathways in their wake. Her parents' love. Her first kiss. Her final moment of fear. All his, now.

No...all HERS.

Rising up from beside the body on the floor, Josie Ballard looks around for matches. When she finds them on the fireplace mantle, she sets fire to furnishings in the living room, then calmly walks out the front door, trusting that the flames will not be bright enough to alert neighbors until she has made her exit. After that, it does not matter if the whole house burns or not, as long as the death within that house has enough of an explanation to satisfy the police.

There was a time that she would have worried about someone identifying the body and seeking out the truth of what happened to it...but experience has taught her, down through the centuries, that such a thing is not possible. The flesh she is leaving behind no longer has an identity that anyone will be able to put a name to, no matter what techniques they apply.

It occurs to her that she should write a poem about this whole experience. As she heads off into the night, she begins to work out what its meter will be.

AUTHOR'S NOTE *for* SOUL MATE

Upstate New York, where our family used to vacation for a few weeks each year, was a place that city folk traditionally escaped to in the summer. It was full of lush greenery, small lakes, and rustic towns: the perfect setting to serve as the hunting grounds of an ancient predator in modern guise.

The arts and crafts festival in this story was inspired by similar events in Berkeley Springs, West Virginia. It's a wonderful little town, full of crafts and antiques, that I would later use as a setting in my Dreamwalker series.

THE LONGEST NIGHT

There is a land where the cold winds blow
and the blood runs chill in mortal veins,
where game is scarce and the hunt is long
and the loneliness drives a man insane.
There is a place where the world is ice,
where even wolves are loathe to roam,
where the earth is white and the sky is black
and the spirit frozen.
I call it home.

The living have given it fearsome names.
The doomed have cursed it with dying breath.
Yet it draws them still, for passion and gold,
this frozen empire whose king is Death.
So they brave the darkness that has no end
and they curse the ice that swallows the day
while madness beckons, invoked by the dark
in a world without sunrise.
I call them prey.

Let the weaklings who must have their fire
huddle close for warmth in the tender south.
I will claim my comfort without a pyre
and I'll wrest my food from Destruction's mouth.
And when nights are empty and hunting bleak,
I'll howl my need as I search for food,
'neath a frozen moon, near to frozen seas,
in a crystalline prairie.
I call it good

For the longest night has come at last
and the sun's extinguished, its glory dead.
But the blackened sky is alight with stars
And the jeweled veils flicker overhead.
Now the smell of blood carries on the wind
like the finest scent of the finest wine,
and time it is frozen, and midnight endures,
in the land that is Winter.
I call it mine.

AUTHOR'S NOTE *for* THE LONGEST NIGHT

This poem is a homage to one of my favorite poets, Robert W. Service. One cold, wintry night I was binge-reading his collected works, enraptured by his descriptions of the arctic winter and its perpetual darkness. At the time, I was deep into my Erciyes project, and so my mind wandered naturally to vampires. What a mixed blessing that kind of locale must be for the undead, I thought: free of the sun, but trapped in a land where sources of blood were few and far between.

It required a poem.

EYE OF THE NEEDLE

TIME TOURS INC, the sign said. The bright, bold letters were scrawled high over a video screen that displayed a sequence of historical panoramas: medieval peasants dancing around a maypole, storm-tossed waves crashing over the bow of a Spanish frigate, toga-clad men and women at a feast, an army of Vikings descending upon a terrified village. Each vignette appeared for ten seconds, then gave way to the next, in seemingly random order. But Christopher McLaren III understood the advertising world well enough to know that there was nothing random about it. An army of psychologists had no doubt been recruited to study every possible sequence of scenes, analyze the emotions that each inspired, and arrange them in the order most likely to get a hesitant visitor to open the door.

For McLaren, the vignettes were uninteresting. Insignificant. He deserved better.

He had put on his best Armani suit for this meeting, a silk tie that cost as much as the average American mortgage payment, and shoes hand-stitched by a 90-year-old artisan in the hills of Italy. Let no one mistake him for a budget-conscious loser, whose financial constraints must be accommodated. He had set his sights on the kind of prize that only a rich man could win, which meant that he must look like a rich man.

It was all about advertising.

The door opened at his approach, revealing a sleek reception room. There was a waiting area to one side, with a stack of tablets on the coffee table: something to read while you waited. He would not be asked to wait, of course. When your worth was measured in as many digits as his was, no one asked you to wait.

He walked up to the reception desk. "Christopher McLaren the third," he told the red-headed receptionist. A video scene displayed over her head shifted from a Druidic ritual to a baroque ball; was that the Sun King? "I have an appointment."

The redhead smiled. "Of course, Mr. McLaren! Welcome to Time Tours. Mr. Fortier will be your agent. Please come this way."

She led him through a common room with half a dozen cramped desks surrounded by racks of tourist brochures. *Witness History in the Making!* one urged. *Secrets of the Past Revealed!* another proclaimed. After that came a quiet hallway flanked by private offices. Much more appropriate to his station in life. She stopped at a door with the name Q. Fortier on it, knocked, then opened it. "Christopher McLaren is here for his appointment, sir."

"Excellent," said the man inside. "Send him in."

Q. Fortier stood as McLaren entered. He was middle-aged, pale-skinned, partly bald, and neatly but not impressively dressed. Likely a man of modest means, which was good for McLaren's purposes. He was standing behind a desk, so McLaren couldn't see his shoes, which was a pity. You could learn a lot about a man from the condition of his shoes.

"Welcome, Mr. McLaren. I'm Quentin Fortier, and I'll be handling your itinerary." He offered his hand; his grip was unimpressive. "Please, have a seat." He waved toward a chair opposite his own. "Will this be your first temporal adventure?"

"It will." The office had no video screens, McLaren noted, but was full of historical artifacts carefully arranged on glass shelves. A Babylonian cuneiform nail, an ivory tusk covered in scrimshaw designs, a number of small yellowed scrolls stacked in a neat pyramid. Some might call the display misleading, as temporal science had not yet advanced to the point where people could bring back souvenirs, but it did give the room an air of significance.

"Time Tours was one of the first travel agencies to take advantage of time travel technology," Fortier told him, "and it remains a leader in the field of temporal tourism. Our equipment is cutting edge and our operators have years of experience, with mandatory recertification at regular intervals. There is no agency that can offer you a better transtemporal experience. Now—" His eyes sparkled "—what jewel of ancient history would you like to witness with your very own eyes? The original Olympics, perhaps? A Shakespearean performance? If you prefer something more primitive we have an outstanding Neolithic package—"

"I would like to attend the Sermon on the Mount," McLaren said.

The smile on the agent's face faltered. "I'm sorry. Do you mean—"

"The one with Jesus. *The meek shall inherit,* and all that." He paused. "I want to be there. I want to hear that famous speech with my own ears."

For a moment the agent was silent. No doubt he was envisioning the fat commission that was about to walk out the door. "I, uh, regret that we can't offer that event at this time. We do have others—"

"That's the only one I'm interested in."

"We have a few other events involving Jesus." Fortier touched his computer screen a few times to bring up the relevant data. "Mostly the Son of God preferred smaller, more intimate gatherings, and those can't be entered into the system…government regulations…ah, here's one that's just been activated." Leaning closer to the screen, he read aloud: *"A fascinating riverside sermon in which various species of fish are presented as models for different types of human behavior."* He looked up. "Or perhaps you would enjoy an action-oriented event more than a speech in an ancient language—"

"I speak ancient Hebrew, Aramaic, Latin, Greek, and Arabic. If you believe Christ would have preached in some other tongue, then tell me which one, and I'll learn that as well." He leaned forward. "I've been preparing for this trip for a very long time, Mr. Fortier. Since the day time tourism began. Back then, I couldn't afford to be among its pioneers. Since then, I've founded and sold three major companies, and spent every waking minute working to amass the knowledge and resources that this outing would require. Now…here I am. Ready to time travel. And there is only one tour that interests me." He leaned back in his chair, steepling his fingers in front of him. "The only question that remains is, what will it cost me?"

Fortier managed to maintain a smile, but his eyes betrayed his frustration. "I'm sorry, but money can't change the science involved. We don't transport your actual body back in time, you understand, only your consciousness, and in order to do that we need a host to receive it. For five minutes you'll override that person's consciousness and view the world through his eyes—see what he sees, feel what he feels. You might even have minimal control over his movements if the connection is strong enough. Sometimes speech is possible. But what that means is that for five minutes your host's brain will be off-limits to every other time traveler, because you are using it." He paused. "Now, imagine that a thousand other time travelers want to view the same event. Five thousand. Ten thousand. They can't all do that, can they? Every event has a finite number of witnesses, Mr. McLaren, and every witness has a finite amount of time when he's present at that location. That's not even taking into account government regulations, which restrict the number of hosts we can claim in any one setting. The majority of spectators need to be from that era, for what I think are obvious reasons."

"All of which means that hosts are *available,*" McLaren pointed out. "You're just not allowed to assign me one."

"The law is what it is." The agent spread his hands apologetically. "Look, Mr. McLaren, all the available slots at the Sermon on the Mount were filled long ago. It was one of the first events in the system that we had to deactivate. Even if I wanted to send you back to that event, I couldn't. Our machinery simply won't accept the coordinates."

McLaren waved off his objection. "Then find someone who can reactivate it. I don't expect that to be a free service, mind you. I'm prepared to pay whatever additional fees are involved." He paused. "I'm also prepared to offer you a generous gratuity for your assistance."

He sighed heavily. "It's not that I don't want to help you—"

"A million dollars."

Fortier's eyes widened. The flow of words ceased.

"The money is waiting right now, ready to be transferred. Help me arrange this tour and it's yours. You could be a millionaire when you wake up tomorrow morning."

For a moment Fortier couldn't seem to find his voice. "Why?" he finally managed. "Why is this one event so important to you?"

McLaren laughed. "Why would I want to hear the speech that is the cornerstone of Western civilization? Why would I want to witness one of the most famous oratory displays that our world has ever known, from Christianity's most revered figure? Why would I want to stand there at that pivotal moment in time, when the fate of our entire world was being decided, and be part of it?" He shook his head, as if the question was too ridiculous to contemplate. "I'll pay whatever it takes, Mr. Fortier. Bribes for technicians, lawyers to help get around government regulations, lobbyists to change those regulations if necessary. If your current equipment won't take me to this event, then I will buy you new equipment. Whatever it takes." He leaned back again. "Now. Either you can help me do this, or I will go to another agency and make them the same offer. And if they fail me, I will go to another agency and try again. Someone, somewhere along the line, will say yes, and I will make that person rich. While you..." He looked around the room with a sigh. "I suppose this isn't too terrible a job to do for the rest of one's life."

Fortier's pale face lost what little color it had. The only thing worse than seeing a million dollars walk out the door was seeing it walk into another mans' office. "I suppose...there might be a way to do it."

Money always wins out in the end, McClaren thought with satisfaction. "And that is?"

"If one of the people who originally reserved a slot at that event failed to attend, his reservation would still be available. He could sell it to you instead."

A triumphant smile spread across McLaren's face. "There! That wasn't so hard, was it?"

Fortier consulted his computer. "The only problem is, no one failed to attend that particular event. The records are quite clear on that point." His brow furrowed in thought. "I suppose that doesn't mean there couldn't *come to be* someone who failed to attend, in a future set of circumstances. If I arranged for an agent to meet with a person who attended this sermon, before he actually did so, and if said agent could convince him to keep his reservation open until today…he could sell it to you for a pre-arranged amount."

"I have money enough to pay any price." McLaren said confidently.

"It might be higher than you think," Fortier warned. "I'm sure you're not the only one who's been after one of those reservations. They've probably changed hands repeatedly, the price increasing each time." He sighed. "Scalping tickets to see God perform. I can't believe that would speak well for a soul on Judgment Day."

McLaren reached into his jacket pocket and pulled out a small leather-bound book. "In here is a list of all the assets I'm willing to assign to this project. Anything that is in there, I'll pay as you advise. Plus the million to you, of course, for facilitating this deal." He put the book down in front of the agent.

Fortier stared at it for a long moment, then reached out and picked it up. "You do realize how ironic this request is, right? Given Jesus's teachings about wealth and all?"

"Irony is the refuge of the weak," McLaren told him. "I look forward to hearing from you."

* * *

Waiting was hard enough for Christopher McLaren under normal circumstances. Waiting for a deal that had not even been proposed yet (what was the proper tense when you were waiting for something to happen in the past?) was agony.

But there was nothing more he could do now. His fate was in the hands of other people, and he could only hope that the bribes he'd paid out and the incentives he'd offered would be sufficient to swing things his way.

On the fireplace mantle of his library was a small, well-worn statue of the Virgin Mary. Years ago it had graced a more modest mantle in his grandmother's home, and every time he saw it now it brought back memories of her reading the words of Jesus to him. She had always stressed the parts that condemned material wealth, as she clearly thought he needed to hear that message. *The men and women who gathered on the Mount to hear Jesus speak were truly blessed. Do you think they rode fancy carriages to get there? Paid merchants, to reserve their spot on the grass? All the money in the world can't buy you that kind of experience, Christopher.*

He had taken it as a personal challenge to prove her wrong.

"Mr. McLaren?"

He turned to see his butler standing in the doorway. "Yes?"

"There's a woman from Temporal Vistas to see you. She's waiting in the reception room."

Temporal Vistas? He'd never done business with that travel agency. Why would one of their people want to talk to him? Unless…was it possible that Fortier had used them to get him a reservation? He could not keep a smile from spreading across his face as he hurried to the reception room to find out. *You see, Grandma? Money can buy anything.*

The woman waiting for him was impeccably dressed in a designer suit, with a Versace handbag tucked under her arm. "Greetings, Mr. McLaren. My name is Sarah Roberts. I'm here to talk to you about your reservation for the Sermon on the Mount."

The smile was twice as broad now. "Please. Have a seat. Can I get you a drink?"

She smiled. "Not necessary. But thank you." She took a tablet out of her handbag and turned on the display. "I've been authorized by my agency to make you an offer." She smiled pleasantly.

"An offer?" Suddenly he was confused. "What kind of offer?"

She read from the tablet. "Mr. Winston Harding, CEO of Greenway Industries, is interested in purchasing your reservation. I'm authorized to negotiate on his behalf." She looked at him. "He's prepared to be quite generous."

For a moment he was at a loss for words. Finally, he managed, "I'm sorry, Ms…"

"Roberts. Sarah Roberts."

"Ms. Roberts. I'm sorry, but I don't understand. You're offering to buy my reservation?"

"Well, technically I'm here to negotiate the terms of purchase with you. The exchange itself wouldn't take place until…" She consulted the tablet. "…September 9th ,2053. You would be obligated to keep the reservation open until then." She offered him the tablet. "A payment schedule is detailed in the proposed contract."

"But…I don't have a reservation to that event."

"Are you sure?" She took the tablet back and scrolled through a few pages. "The instructions are right here: *Offer terms at 604 5th Avenue, Penthouse Suite, August 22nd.*"

"It's only the 21st," he pointed out.

"Oh." Her eyes grew wide. "Oh. I'm so terribly sorry. That's the trouble with transtemporal contracts, you know. Communication can be so glitchy." She turned the tablet off and slid it back into her purse. "Forgive me for taking up your time. I'll see that the offer is rescheduled."

Suddenly the full significance of her visit hit home. Just as he had sent people back in time to negotiate with those who had an open reservation to the event in Galilee, someone from the future was now sending agents back to negotiate with him. Which could mean only one thing: he was going to get his booking!

At 2:13 P.M the next day he received official notice from his travel agent: five minutes of host time had been reserved for him at the Sermon on the Mount. He barely had time to open a celebratory bottle of champagne before a temporal agent showed up to try to buy the reservation from him. By 3:30 there was a long line of people outside his front door, each one from a different travel agent from the future, representing a different wealthy client.

Few pleasures in life were sweeter than knowing you had something others wanted. He thoroughly enjoyed saying no.

* * *

Heat: that was the first thing he became aware of. Dry heat, sauna intensity, penetrating every cell of his flesh. Then a blazing light that seared his eyelids, painful in its intensity. Given that his body was actually floating in a room-temperature sensory deprivation tank, in total darkness, the sensations were fascinating.

You will be disoriented when you first arrive. There may be some sensory distortion. This is completely normal. The initial adjustment can take as long as half a minute—which will seem like an eternity while it's happening—but just be patient. Focus on the body you are in. Breathe in, breathe out. Things will come into focus soon enough. The clock will not start on your excursion until consciousness transfer is complete.

A vintage Lamborghini roadster. That's what this little excursion was costing him. Also a luxury condo in Manhattan and ten million dollars. All in all, not a bad deal. McLaren had certainly been prepared to pay more. But it turned out the one man willing to sell his reservation wasn't a savvy business mogul looking to bankroll a new empire. He was just a normal, everyday guy, successful enough to have been able to buy a temporal ticket when the technology was first launched, smart enough to realize that the combination of limited supply and unlimited demand would soon send the value of that ticket soaring. While other high-demand reservations passed from hand to hand, billionaires struggling to bribe and negotiate and coerce their way into the temporal queue, he had simply waited patiently for the right offer to come along. It was the vintage Lamborghini that had ultimately tipped the scales in McLaren's favor. Apparently this guy loved cars.

Lying in the darkness-that-was-not-dark, baking in the heat-that-was-not-real, he reviewed details from his orientation. *Your control over the host body will be minimal. You will be able to initiate small motions, but nothing more; you may or may not be able to speak. Remember that your role is to be that of an observer, not an active participant. Any attempt to alter the flow of history will be detected by our system and is a felony under temporal law.*

A twinge of pain suddenly shot up his leg. That was odd. They hadn't warned him to expect any pain. The heat was growing stronger now, and his skin felt odd, as if his body was coated in something thick and greasy. There was salt on his lips—

And suddenly he was standing in the open air, blinking against the brightness of the sun. The pain in his left leg was searing. Something hard and coarse was sticking into his left underarm, scraping raw flesh. Not exactly the arrival he'd hoped for.

But he was here!

As his eyes adjusted to the brightness, he could make out details of a land baked in heat and crowded with people. Everything seemed oddly fuzzy, though. He could see that the hillside he was standing on was terraced, and could make out a few distant figures more brightly dressed than the earth-toned crowd surrounding him, but not much else. He squinted, trying to bring the scene into better focus. In the distance, at the peak of the hill, was a single figure. Maybe Jesus? The man was too far away—and too fuzzy—for McLaren to tell. As for whatever speech the man was making, the few words that were loud enough for McLaren to hear were nearly incomprehensible. Jesus might have been speaking one of the languages McLaren knew, but if so, it was an unfamiliar dialect.

The pain in his leg was agonizing. He looked down and discovered that the limb was withered and twisted; the crude crutch poking into his underarm was all that was keeping him upright. The pain was increasing with each passing moment, and as he tried to shift position to ease the pressure on his leg, memories associated with that pain flooded his mind. They had warned him back in the 21st century that something like this might happen.

You will share the physical experience of your host, and perhaps some of his mental essence as well. He will not be banished from the scene, but will be present in the back of your mind in a sleep-like state, perceiving bits of his surroundings as if in a dream. Fragments of his memories may surface, and will become available to you.

It had all sounded interesting enough back in the 21st century, but when your host had lived for years in brutal poverty and agonizing pain, his memories were nothing to celebrate. Now they were filling McLaren's brain, making it hard to think about anything else. He tried focusing on his surroundings—he only had five minutes here, after all—fixing on one fuzzy point after another, trying to bring things into sharper focus. Then suddenly he realized why everything looked so unclear. His host was *nearsighted*.

"Fuck!" The expletive escaped his lips before he could stop it.

Most of the crowd didn't seem to notice, but one man turned back to look at him. "Could have been worse," he said in a low voice, in English. "They could have assigned you a leper."

Startled, McLaren nearly lost his balance. The homemade crutch stabbed him in his underarm, prompting a fresh wave of pain. He focused on breathing for a moment, to steady himself—*slowly in, slowly out*—then cleared his throat to test how much physical control he had. Finally he attempted to speak. "That's not exactly comforting." The voice didn't sound like his, but at least he could talk.

The man's shoulders twitched slightly; perhaps he was trying to shrug. "People come here in hopes of being healed. It's hard to begrudge them that."

"Time travel's a crap shoot," someone on McLaren's other side observed, startling him yet again.

A man nearby muttered something in Spanish.

A woman, sotto voce in English, said, "Always check the location of your seat before purchasing your ticket." She chuckled.

"Shhh!" A woman ahead of them turned back to glare. "Some of us are trying to hear the sermon!"

"Good luck with that," someone else muttered.

More and more people were looking in his direction now, and he could pick out many whose stiff, minimalist movements suggested they were not in full control of their bodies. In fact, the majority of people near him seemed to be moving in that manner. Good God, were they *all* time travelers? If so, there were far more tourists at this location than regulations allowed. But then, had he not tried to bribe Fortier to defy those very regulations? Clearly others had done the same. Multiply those efforts a thousandfold, with an endless flow of tourists trying to bribe their way back in time to this one moment, and the result was an event so overloaded with spectators that few locals would actually witness it. And the implications of that were stunning. Might there come a day when people would trade temporal reservations to prime events like they now traded material goods? Would the price of a 1% share in the Gettysburg Address be treated as a commodity—speculated upon, bid for, listed on the New York Stock Exchange? If so, that would be ironically tragic, for those who had the greatest interest in witnessing such events would be the least likely to do so. A college professor whose entire life had been dedicated to studying the Norman Conquest wouldn't be able to afford a ticket to see the event unfold; devotees of a holy man would not be able to witness his teachings. History would become a playground of the rich and powerful, with scholars and pilgrims left out in the cold.

And what about those locals who might have witnessed the event, had tourists from the future not interfered? Their awareness of it would be little more than a hazy dream, filtered through a stranger's mind. History must be full of pivotal events like this one, which few locals actually witnessed. How might the world had been different if more people from the past had actually heard this sermon by Jesus? Or the Gettysburg Address? Or Frederick Douglass' Fourth of July speech? It was almost more than a mind could grasp.

Suddenly the heat was too much for him. And the pain. His crippled leg gave way, and he did not have enough motor control to save himself from falling. His head struck the ground hard, which made the whole world spin around him. Alien emotions filled his head, crowding out his thoughts. Pain. Desperation. The exhaustion of a man who had reached the end of physical endurance. McClaren fought back. He tried to hold onto his own identity and not lose himself in another man's life. But it was impossible. The despair in those memories was too strong. He was drowning in it.

But something also stirred in his mind that was not despair, and he clung to it like a lifeline. It was a gentle emotion, such as he would not have expected this suffering man to know, yet it was more powerful than the pain in his body or the exhaustion of his spirit. Grateful for the reprieve, McClaren embraced it. And slowly, as it refreshed his soul, he realized what it was.

Hope.

Such a fragile spark, amidst so much suffering! This was the core of his host's soul: not a driving, aggressive strength, such as McClaren had always admired, but something subtler, and perhaps more even powerful. It was an unfamiliar sensation, so it took him a moment to give it a name.

Faith.

This was what had had brought the crippled man here: not just a quest for physical healing, but for spiritual peace. And now here this pilgrim was, surrendering his most precious experience to another, all for the price of a fancy car and a penthouse condo. But that faith was still inside him, McClaren realized. It would always be inside him. Such a thing could not be bought, borrowed, stolen, or destroyed.

For the first time in his life, McClaren understood.

On the shores of Galilee, Christopher McLaren III shut his borrowed eyes, and let the faith of a crippled stranger sweep him away. The 2.4 minutes remaining seemed to last forever, yet were over in an instant. His temporal connection began to fade, returning him to his normal world. His normal life. He could feel another time traveler slipping into that malformed body in his place, drawing a new veil before those ancient, nearsightded eyes. How much had this new tourist paid for this host's time? Not nearly as much as the host was being asked to pay.

Alone in the darkness of the deprivation tank, McClaren wept for him.

AUTHOR'S NOTE *for* EYE OF THE NEEDLE

This story was already taking shape in my head when Joshua Palmatier invited me to contribute to his upcoming anthology, TEMPORALLY DISCONNECTED. Its combination of humor, social commentary, and philosophical speculation was inspired by the stories that first drew me to science fiction.

For those not familiar with the quote the title refers to, it is from the Book of Matthew: "It is easier for a camel to go through the eye of a needle, than for a rich man to enter into the kingdom of God." Similar imagery appears in the Talmud and the Quran.

THE DREAMING KIND

There was a time between sunset and twilight when the wall between the worlds grew thin; when, if one was watching—if one knew how to watch—the dark little creatures of the dreamworld could be seen slithering through.

The one called Hunter-in-Darkness knew how to watch.

The time would come just before true darkness fell, in that moment when night and day were most precariously balanced. It would last for just a few seconds (but that was long enough), and then the passage would close again, and the things which had come from *there* to *here* must now remain *here* forever.

He never failed to watch it happen, once he had learned how. And he never hunted until after it was over. The shadowy dream-creatures fascinated him. He had seen such things in the dreamworld, of course, and had hunted them there; to do so was a cat-custom as old as the world itself. But here they seemed…wrong, somehow. As if passage into the waking world had weakened them. Their inner light was dim, often flickering, and their edges dissolved as the wind brushed against them, trailing off into thin wisps of fog. They came in a thousand shapes, no two alike: from tapering worms of amber-gray mist to crab-like clots of crimson smoke that scuttled over unseen pebbles and stones. All of them wrong.

He had hunted them once, in his kittenhood, but had quickly

learned the futility of such action. In the world of dreams such creatures had substance and might be hunted, slain, and eaten, but in the waking lands they were wraithlike and could not be harmed, either by claw or fang. One was left with only a foul-smelling residue where contact should have been made, a bitter reminder that *something* had not been caught. It was better to leave such hunting to one's dream-self, and devote the waking hours to capturing more substantial prey.

Tonight he would hunt in the human lands. The moonless night was perfect for it, the darkness so thick that he could feel it brush against his coat, black against black in the chill autumn wind. There was the outer fence to deal with, of course, but that was no real obstacle. Like a neuter's spray it lacked any real authority; his people had scratched their way under it or climbed over it so often that it looked—and smelled—like a thoroughfare. He found a well-worn channel that cut under the wirework and crawled through it easily, into the home turf of the same two-footed creatures who had once tried to kill him.

And there he found prey. He saw it first, a moving point of bodylight against the ebony darkness. Mouse? He was downwind of it, and began a careful approach. Soon the scent came to him, warm and promising, confirming his guess: mouse. He took each step carefully, avoiding the dry leaves that were scattered across the field, whose crunching might give him away. Hunting in the autumn was always a challenge.

Suddenly his prey pricked up its tiny ears, alert. He froze. Time passed. He was as motionless as the earth itself. The mouse looked around, then moved two steps closer to a patch of ivy. Still Hunter-in-Darkness did not move. Finally his prey relaxed, then began nosing down among the fallen leaves for food. The hunter dared a slow step forward, then another one. The mouse was in plain view now, and the wisps of bodylight that clung to its coat rippled across its fur, making it easy to see.

It would hear him when he leapt, he knew, and would probably dart for cover. He guessed that it would run off in *that* direction, and then try to evade him *there*....

Strong hind legs propelled him into the air, straight as an arrow. The mouse ran in exactly the direction he had anticipated. An instant later he was upon it, his claws dug firmly into its shoulder, his teeth closing joyously about the tiny neck. Its bodylight flickered in his nostrils as he subdued it, and when he tired of its struggles, he killed it, ate it, and left the scraps, faintly glowing, upon a pile of gold-edged leaves. He knew from experience that the light of its life would take a while to fade completely; not until dawn would the last of it drift off.

It was then that he became aware that something was watching him.

He turned quickly. Ears flattened, claws unsheathed, he was ready for whatever battle the intrusion required. But all he saw was a dream-creature, its form glowing brightly against night's backdrop: an unwholesome shape, half fish and half slug, with a gaping, tooth-ringed mouth at the forward end. He moved out of its way, his fur bristling, and although he made a token effort to smooth the hairs down with his tongue, his nerves were on edge; the ugly thing had frightened him.

But it had no interest in feline company. It floated past him, moving against the breeze, until it came to the location of his recent meal. And then it paused, as though considering its next action. He felt himself growl, in loathing and in fear. Though the thing had no scent, its aura was decidedly threatening; it took all his self-control not to turn and run from it.

It hovered over the mouse carcass for a long while, its foggy flesh pulsing. And then it settled upon the body, leechlike, its round mouth fastened to what was left of the head. Horrified, Hunter-in-Darkness watched it feed. No flesh passed into the dream-creature, but the light contained within the carrion slowly began to fade. Sparks shivered weakly above the corpse, then were extinguished. Within a short time there was only the bodylight of the leech thing—and Hunter himself—to see by.

Fear outweighed curiosity at last, and Hunter-in-Darkness turned and ran.

* * *

The old farmhouse, Miles noted, was just as he had expected it to be, no more and no less. His old college roommate had decided to renovate it, but the job was only half finished, and would probably remain that way forever. Wesley McGillis had a tendency to grow bored with any project once he had mastered the skills necessary to complete it, and this house was no exception. A pity. The old building had promise. Maybe Wes' daughter, who had recently moved in with him, would motivate him to finish the project.

There was no obvious place to park, so he just pulled into the yard. Wes was waiting on the porch, a broad grin spreading across his face, and damn him, he hadn't changed a bit since the last they'd met! Miles looked older, that was certain. For a brief instant he was jealous.

"How do you like it?" Wes asked, stepping down from the porch. A sweeping gesture encompassed the house, the grounds, and even the gleaming white citadel of Bell & Hammond's research facility in the distance. "Nice, eh?"

"Cold." Miles was wearing a jacket better suited to Georgia weather than this northern climate. "Give me the southlands, any day." He retrieved his duffel bag from his trunk and started toward the house.

"Here, I'll take that." Wes reached for the bag, and they had a brief tussle over it, just like they used to do in college. God, it brought back memories! Finally Wes managed to pull it out of his hand. "You're sounding like them, you know that?"

"Who?"

"Southerners. Never thought you would." Wes led him up the stairs of the weathered porch, to a screen door that was obviously new. "Elsa sands her love, wishes she could be here. Some business down at NIMH. I'll tell you all about it once you're settled in. Odd stuff, really." Opening the door, he waved Miles through. "Watch out for the cats," he warned.

As if on cue, a gray tabby bolted toward the door. Wes blocked its way with his foot, pushing Miles into a simply furnished kitchen as he pulled the screen door shut behind them. The cat yowled once—a token protest—and then disappeared into a nearby shadow.

Adjoining the kitchen was a common room, in which a crackling fire had been lit, taking the edge off the autumn chill. Wesley gestured toward the sitting area in front of it. "Make yourself comfortable while I stow your gear. There's hot water on for coffee or tea, your choice. Be back in a minute." He headed up the stairs.

Miles had just enough time to notice that the legs of the rocker were scarred and its cover fringed by the repeated application of animal claws, when a cry of "Downstairs, damn you!" resonated from the second floor, and a small ball of fur flew down the stairs. Black from head to tail, with white socks on three of its feet, the small cat dashed into the center of the room and then stopped suddenly, as if startled by something. Hesitantly Miles extended one finger toward it; he was a dog man himself, awkward around felines, but if the cat was Wes' pet he would at least make an attempt to be friendly.

The cat turned to face him, and its eyes grew wide. Hissing, it drew back. Its long, thick fur was standing on end, an effect that was at once ludicrous and unnerving. The tiny throat spasmed, and a roaring sound issued from the cat's mouth that was proof of its kinship to lions.

Shaken, Miles withdrew his hand. Any sound or quick movement seemed to agitate the tiny beast even more, so he made himself very quiet and very small, and waited for Wes to return and save him.

From the top of the stairs came the sound of footsteps as Wes descended. "I've given you the front room; it's somewhat small, but the best restored. I think—"

He stopped as reached the bottom of the stairs and took in the tableau—*tiny cat vs. professor of philosophy*—in an amused glance. "Calm down, Miles. He isn't going to attack you. I promise."

"But when I moved toward it—"

"Take a look at his eyes. He isnt even looking at you."

Miles looked at the cat again, and realized that Wes was right. Its eyes were fixed on some point slightly to the left of him, in what looked like empty space. "Then what the hell is its problem?"

Wes sighed. "Not an easy question to answer. l suppose I should tell you about Elsa's project, since you're going to be living with the results of it while you're here. That's what she's gone to talk to the people down south about."

"A cat?"

"Four cats. And two litters before that, which were destroyed soon after birth. These are the first that were allowed to grow to adulthood, and sometimes I'm not sure that was a good idea. Coffee?"

"Please."

"Cream? Sugar?"

"Stark naked." Concern for his health had weaned him from additives; he had a tendency to put on weight. As Wes left to make the coffee, he asked nervously, "It's not dangerous, is it?"

"What, the coffee?" Wes laughed in the kitchen. "They're too small to do us any real damage. Though 1 imagine mice feel differently."

The cat was still puffed up, though its roar had quieted somewhat. *I didn't know they could make noises like that.* "What's it looking at? What's it afraid of?" To him it seemed there was nothing else in the room, yet the cat was obviously responding to something. By watching it closely he could tell where that *something* was, but he had no clue as to its nature.

Wes returned with two cups of steaming coffee, and was about to speak when the cat suddenly leaped straight up into the air, yowling as if something had clawed it. It bolted for the dark space under an easy chair and dove into it, its whole body shivering with terror. A moment later its eyes were visible, two glowing embers in shadow, and they scanned the room anxiously.

"I guess I'd better explain," Wes offered, as he handed him his coffee. It was an understatement as far as Miles was concerned. "Elsa's division has been experimenting with small animals for some time now, in connection with their study of vision development in premature infants. They used gene splicing to produce specimens with specific visual handicaps. One of her projects involved splicing a feline litter for improved chromatic sensitivity, a routine operation that should have had routine results. Instead it produced a set of four kittens that, from the moment they opened their eyes, exhibited all the symptoms of human schizophrenia." Wes sipped his coffee. "They were put to sleep. And she tried again. Same result. By then she had checked and double-checked every genetic factor, and an autopsy was performed on every corpse. But all their investigative methods confirmed that the only change was in the color sensitivity of the cat's visual apparatus; there was no indication of any change in the brain itself to explain such dramatic behavior. As a final experiment, they let the last four live." Wes nodded toward the glowing eyes under the chair. "She talked me into taking them in so that they could have some kind of normal upbringing. She wanted to see if they would fare better here than in a lab." Another sip. "We sterilized them, of course. Can't have mutants contaminating the local gene pool."

"Did it help?"

"See for yourself." A black-tailed tabby was slinking into the room, stalking something that Miles couldn't see. A moment later it hissed and ran out again. "Not that most cats don't have imaginary playmates...but rarely do they display such hostility toward them. Then Elsa was contacted by someone at NIMH, who invited her to come down and share her notes with them. They want to compare her observations with those of human subjects with various mental disorders. Meanwhile..." He shrugged toward the small black cat, which was only just now extricating itself from its shadowy fortress. "I've got three of these to contend with. Surprisingly intelligent little beasts when they're not acting bonkers. They're quite a handful."

"Three?" Miles frowned. "I thought you said there were four."

"There were. But one got out of the house before we had them neutered, and..." He sighed heavily. "We couldn't lure it back, and we definitely couldn't let it remain free. So we had to hunt it down. A friend of Elsa's did it, actually. Shot him right in the head. The poor thing had less than a day of freedom." He paused. "We didn't report it. Didn't want to risk Elsa's license, you understand? So it's a litter of three, now, as far as the records are concerned. Always has been."

The small black cat walked with leisurely grace to the nearest chair, climbed into it, and proceeded to wash itself. *Just like a real cat*, Miles thought. Only it wasn't. Science had altered it. *Non-cat. Anti-cat.* He had never approved of gene-splicing animals, and now he knew why. Too much DNA, and far too little knowledge. Of course, you could probably splice dogs safely. Dogs were predictable.

Comprehensible. Cats were…

He looked at the small black feline and shivered.

…*Alien.*

* * *

They were gathering in the human lands. Dozens of them, moonbright beneath the evening sky. Not the dream-creatures he had hunted as a kitten, his paws passing through their flesh as if through smoke. These were large ones, grotesque ones. Like the dream-creature which had claimed his prey, they stank of *wrongness,* of decay; they frightened him, and only as he watched them gather about the tall white building did he finally admit that he was seeing more of them there every night, as if something in the white building was calling to them.

That the nights were growing colder didn't help matters. He was protected from winter's chill by a thick coat of fur, but his paws were unaccustomed to treading frozen ground, and the scar which cut across his face, marking the place where a bullet once struck him, ached painfully when the temperature dropped too low. Both played havoc with his temper. When the dream-creatures approached he would swipe at them, claws extended, even though he knew that no waking creature could hurt them. He tried anyway, giving vent to his irritation and discomfort, and snarled in frustration when his paw passed through them. He had hunted them in the dreamlands and never understood why here, in the waking world, they were intangible; now the situation was becoming intolerable, as they followed him during his hunt and claimed his kill, and he was powerless to drive them away.

He hungered to visit the white building, to see why all the dream-creatures were so interested in it. But in the fields surrounding it, where humans had cropped the grass to indecent shortness and removed every last bit of cover, he would have to be wary. He knew the power of humans all too well, and was not anxious to test it. Soon after his escape from a smaller building they had hunted him like prey, and when they got close enough there was ear-splitting thunder, and a searing pain that blinded him; his head struck rock as he fell, and he tumbled down into a narrow crevice. Then the shadowlands had claimed him for a time. He was half-dead when he awoke, and barely managed to climb out of the tight space and get to a place where he could heal safely. No, he was anxious to seek out human company.

But the dream-creatures were gathering around that building for a reason. And he needed to know why.

Carefully he slid along the short grass, his body low to the ground, inching his way slowly forward. The tall white building had its own fence, taller and more formidable than the one at the edge of the woods. There were no trees here to offer him a way over, nor any visible pathway scratched beneath it. He decided to climb the fence itself, and took a running leap to gain as much height as possible. But his paws were burned as they struck the wire, a searing pain that made his whole body spasm. He lost hold of the wire and went crashing down to the ground, with no time to right himself. He yowled as he hit the hard-packed earth and lay there, stunned, his paws on fire, his body half-paralyzed from shock.

This was not like the other fence. This one had human magic in it, and like the thunder which had struck him down before, it was deadly. If he had clung to it any longer he might have died; only his fall had saved him.

Humbled, he pulled himself onto his feet. His paws felt raw and his legs were weak and trembling, but he made them carry him westward, to the nearest shelter, a dense evergreen brush. There, with spiny leaves for shelter, he could examine and cleanse his wounds. He passed a scent-mark along the way but ignored it; he lacked the strength to return to his own territory, and so must risk the sin of trespass. Exhausted, his flesh numb where the fence had burned him, he finally collapsed into a bed of dried needles, hoping that whatever cat had marked this place was someplace far away, patrolling the opposite border of its territory. He had no strength to fight.

He was just about to slip into the dreamlands when a rustling awoke him. In an instant he was fully awake and standing tall, fur puffed out, pain shooting through all his legs but looking like he was ready for battle. Woe betide the cat that picked a fight with him, even when he was wounded! Hopefully the appearance of strength would be enough to scare off trouble, because he really didn't feel like fighting.

The rustling grew louder, and at last a tiny head peeked out from between two branches, all eyes and whiskers. Then a second appeared, equally small. The wind carried kitten-scent to him, and his fur settled down a bit. Such tiny cats were no threat to him.

Then a third tiny face appeared, and he forgot all else in his wonder. For the green flame that burned in its eyes was like his own bodylight, and he knew by how it picked its way through the brush that it could see in the darkness the same way he could. Green fire played along its black fur as it sauntered up to him, playful and curious. He was about to touch noses with it when a dream-creature came into view; with a yelp the tiny kitten bounded after it. The kitten could see them in the waking world! Hunter-in-Darkness was stunned. In all his time in the woods, he had never met another cat who could do that.

He was preparing to follow the youngster when another scent came to him, this one adult and hostile. He turned, and found himself facing an enraged female. A paw swipe mere inches from his face drove him back a step; he found himself loathe to do battle with an angry mother, and stepped back yet again as she lunged at him. Finally, with no thought for dignity, he turned and ran, and he continued until his injured paws hurt so much he had to stop. He dared to turn around and look behind him, then, and was relieved to see she was no longer following. Off collecting her kittens, no doubt. Thankful for her maternal instinct, he fell to the ground and started licking his wounds anew.

What was it that seemed so familiar about that female? Her scent was familiar, but not quite right. He had known another female once, in the time of warmth and rain, and her scent had been similar, but stronger, sweeter. More welcoming. That female had swiped at him too, but consorts often did that after mating. Could this be the same cat?

Warmed by the memory of his spring courting, he found himself a safe place to sleep, and let the shadowlands carry him away, so that his body could do its healing in peace.

* * *

Miles looked up at the gleaming white building, the cold blue light of morning playing across its upper ramparts. "So this is it?"

"Indeed it is. Home of my pet project. And thank God for Bell & Hammond, because I couldn't have covered the cost of this through the standard grants. Not given how long it might be before we get any publishable results." He showed his pass to the guards, and they ran it through a reader and then returned it to him. They looked at Miles' driver's license, then gave him a lanyard with a temporary pass. "This way," Wes said, pulling open a heavy steel door.

The corridors of the Bell & Hammond facility were as clean and sterile as the outside. Miles wondered how his friend, who tended toward a cluttered lifestyle, could stand the place.

At last they came to Wes' computer lab, with a separate key card to open it. "Welcome to the Eden project," he announced, throwing open the door with a flourish.

For paradise, it was remarkably unimpressive. True, there were computers along all four walls and a shoulder-high island in the room's center, but they were of the same sleek design which marked the entire complex, offering little hint of why they were here, or what they were doing.

"What do you think?" Wes asked, grinning.

"You have a lot of hardware," Miles allowed. "More than that will require an explanation."

"Of course, of course. But where do I start?" Wes looked proudly around the room; this project was his brainchild, Miles knew, in every sense of the word. "About five billion years ago the first life appeared on Earth. Here, in this room, I mean to replicate the process. How's that?"

Miles blinked. "You're kidding me, right? You want to create life? In this room?"

Wes nodded. "We know what the Earth was like when life first appeared. But the odds of all the right factors coming together in just the right way must have been infitesmally small, because as far as we know, it never happened again. Science has struggled to understand that moment. We have made viruses, crafted custom bacteria, played God with some of the higher species... but always there was a seed of life that we started with, some fragment of a living entity that we used to get it all going.What I proposed was starting from scratch. Creating life out of nothing." His eyes were sparkling with the wild energy that Miles remembered from their college days " Is that crazy enough? Will you write it all off as another eccentricity of mine—God knows, I have enough of them—or do you want to hear the details?"

It did sound crazy, but his curiosity had been piqued. "If you can convince a company like Bell & Hammond that you're not insane, I can certainly listen. Go on."

Wes placed a loving hand on the central island, stroking it as one might a beloved child. "We know approximately when life first appeared. We know the conditions of the Earth during that time, from its composition to its surface temperature, even the intensity of the sun, and can work out all the other relevant details of the environment, down to the smallest detail. Somewhere in all that data is the single set of conditions that permitted a combination of amino acids to become self-replicating—which is the bottom-line definition of life as we know it.

"Scientists have tried to develop some algorithm that would reveal those conditions to us, but to no avail. They've tried to reason their way backwards to that moment six ways from Sunday—reverse engineering Creation, if you will—and had no success whatsoever. All I proposed was to let computers do what they do best: go through reams of data until they find something promising, and then test it in all its permutations. These machines"—he indicated the wall-to-wall computer banks—"mathematically reproduce all possible conditions of the Earth during that period. Every conceivable variable is accounted for. Sunspots, volcanic activity, meteoric impact, tectonic drift...The sheer mass of data is beyond anything that a team of human beings could analyze in a lifetime. Hell, a thousand lifetimes!

Only computers can handle this type of operation. And it may take decades before we have any kind of an answer."

"I'm surprised you were able to get funding."

"No shit," he agreed. "But Bell & Hammond must see potential profit in it, or they wouldn't be footing the bill." He looked around the room with pride. "It's a structured trial-and-error system with an almost infinite database. I tried not to prejudice it with any human expectations. I just feed it data and let it run. As soon as it comes up with a set of conditions conducive to the chemical processes we need, the system will initiate a test program that will reproduce those exact conditions. Mathematically, of course. That part is automatic." His eyes were gleaming, his voice more full of life than Miles ever remembered it. "I dream of coming in here and discovering that the testing sequence has already started."

Miles drew in a deep breath. "So one might say, in a purely mathematical sense, that the process of creating life has already begun."

"Exactly." Wes grinned.

His mouth tightened. "It's a good thing you're not a religious man, Wes."

"Why? Do you think I would have done things differently, in that case?"

"Well, if there is such a thing as a soul, and if all living creatures have one…" Miles walked up to the central island and touched a hand to its surface. Cold. That surprised him. Shouldn't the creation of life feel warmer? "Where will your new soul come from, when you create this living entity? Must you create that, too? Or is there some kind of disembodied consciousness already in existence, that would bond with your creation? Move in and take up housekeeping, as it were? A religious man might worry about that—and about its possible source."

Wes snorted. "You're getting morbid in your old age, Miles. The universe is filled with souls, old and new. Or so say our high priests."

"But once it wasn't so. And your machines are reproducing those very conditions." He shrugged. "It's food for thought, anyway."

"Sometimes I imagine I can feel it happening," Wes murmured. "I stand here, and it's like I can sense the process coming to fruition. Like something is almost—but not quite—ready. The final stage could begin any minute now, maybe while we're talking here. Am I crazy, Miles?"

"Always have been."

"Can you feel it, I mean. The incipient...the *incipience* of it."

"All I feel is tired. And a bit of a headache." He touched a hand to his forehead, wondering at the weakness that had suddenly come over him. "I'm afraid you've quite overwhelmed me, Wes. I need some time to process all this."

Wes' eyes narrowed. "You all right? You look a bit pale."

"Just tired, I think. It was a long drive. And this really is quite overwhelming." He rubbed his forehead, where the worst of the tiredness seemed to be centered. "The philosophical implications really are staggering. Give me time, Wes. And a good lunch. Suddenly I feel pretty hungry."

His ex-roommate smiled as he led the way out. "Then a short nap, eh? You never were a morning person."

Miles snorted. "Took you thirty years to notice..."

* * *

Hunter-in-Darkness watched from the forest's edge as the two men exited the building, keeping to the shadows so that they wouldn't see him. Even from a distance he could not fail to notice the crablike shape which sat atop the shorter man's head. It had tentacles pressed to the man's upper face, and now and then the man swatted at it as though he could sense its presence. But his hand passed right through it.

Chilled despite the morning's warmth, Hunter-in-Darkness headed back into the depths of the forest.

He needed to think.

* * *

Dear Dad—

Well, I'll be staying down here longer than originally planned, but didn't we think that might happen? There's so much to tell you that I hardly know where to start; suffice it to say that we've come up with some interesting hypotheses to explain our cats' behavior.

So far, the most promising theory involves some kind of dream disturbance. Dr. Langsdon pulled a video for me, of cats that had been treated so that while they dreamed their motor activity wasn't inhibited, as it usually is during sleep. The result was that they acted out their dreams, and—you guessed it—the resulting behavior was very similar to that of our little houseguests. More to come on that, but I really should wait until I get home, to tell you in person. It's all so very exciting!

The upshot of all this is that I won't be leaving until next Sunday at the earliest. Does that mean I miss seeing Miles? Tell him to stop off in Maryland if he drives home earlier than that, and I'll take him to lunch. Or dinner.

Pet the beasts for me.
Elsa.

* * *

The dreamworld was unusually dark tonight, which made the firesprites even more distracting than usual. Hunter-in-Darkness stopped for a moment, watching them burst into life and dart across leafless branches, then disappear a moment later, swallowed by darkness. Overhead, the cold, dead trees of the shadowland forest wove a spiderweb canopy of jagged black branches, and the shifting light of the sprites created moving shadows that made the whole sky seem alive. It was all familiar to him. But there was a smell in the air tonight that did not belong, a hint of foulness that the wind carried to him, that made his lips draw back from his teeth and brought a hiss of disgust to his throat. He turned around to escape it, to search for prey elsewhere.

Then, suddenly, he remembered.

Like all cats, he spent his dream time hunting in the perpetual twilight of the shadowlands, perfecting his skills in a world that demanded perfection in timing and concentration. And like all cats—until tonight—he had passed from one world to the other without thought, sinking into the dreaming world without awareness, rising from it briefly to smooth his fur, then passing back into dreaming once more, without thought or effort. In and out again, in a rhythm as ancient and as natural as breathing.

But tonight was different. Tonight he suddenly was aware of both worlds at once. He understood that while he was hunting in this place, he was also sleeping in a leaf-cushioned hollow in the waking world. He struggled to sort it all out in his head, and to understand why such double awareness had come to him. Was it caused by the same magic that allowed the dream-creatures to cross into the waking lands? Something was changing that affected both worlds, and it did not smell right.

He turned toward the source of the foul smell, drawing the scent into the roof of his mouth in order to savor it fully. Images of the dream-creatures came to him, clumps of fog that had left the same foulness in his mouth. This was the stink of their wrongness, and his survival instinct urged him to flee from it. But tonight he had the strength of both worlds behind him, and he would not run. These things had fouled his territory, ignored his markings, and despoiled his kill. If he failed to deal with them here, where they were vulnerable, he might wind up driven from his own territory.

With the stealth of a seasoned hunter he crept slowly toward the source of the odor. All about him new firesprites burst to life, danced in fiery zigzags, and were consumed by darkness; by their light he picked his way across the lifeless roots of the black forest, letting his sense of smell guide him. Gradually the foul odor grew stronger, and its message made his hackles rise. *Turn back. Run away. This place is not for you.*

He ignored it.

Suddenly he heard a high-pitched howl of distress, ending in a yelp that he recognized. But that voice belonged to the waking world. How could it be here? For a moment he stood still, frozen by indecision. Then the cry came again, a terrible yowling of pain and fear that made hesitation unthinkable. In his mind's eye a tiny black kitten was crying for help, its bright green eyes fading. He began to run toward the sound.

He came into the clearing suddenly, and had to use all his claws to brake to a stop. It was there. The kitten. The same one he had met in the waking lands, whose fiery gaze had so impressed him. *They* were there as well, the same foul dream-creatures that had crossed into the waking world and driven him from his kill. They had downed the kitten and were feeding on it. Suckers and teeth were affixed to its trembling body, and the dream-creatures pulsed with light as they fed. Hunter-in-Darkness could see the crimson glitter of blood across the tiny cat's jet-black fur.

Rage consumed him. He abandoned thought, becoming a creature of blind action. One leap and he was upon the nearest, a fish-like thing with claws, fins, and a long spiked tail. Here in the shadowlands the creatures had physical substance, and he tore into this one with relish. So quickly did he dispatch it that the others were just beginning to react when he chose his next victim. This was not hunting, but killing, plain and simple, and he took no pleasure in it. A snake-like creature with silver spines drew itself up to fight; he clawed at its face before it got a chance to position itself effectively, and was rewarded with a shower of foul-smelling blood across his paw and chest. Teeth bit into his hind leg, but he kicked out savagely and they were gone. There were more dream-creatures than he could count, but he was a whirlwind of teeth and claws and fury, and at last, hissing their displeasure, the survivors fled the scene of battle.

He took no time to lick his wounds, but looked around for the injured kitten. It had crawled off during the battle, leaving a thin trail of blood behind it. So dim was its bodylight that he nearly lost the little creature, but he let his sense of smell guide him, and finally found the shivering infant, a tiny ball of wet fur that hissed weakly as he approached it. It was badly injured, and shaking from terror. And no wonder! One of the advantages of hunting in the shadowlands was that prey didn't usually fight back. The thought that the dream-creatures could do this to a cat—*would* do this to a cat—was chilling.

Gently he nuzzled the youngster, and began to lick its wounds clean of blood and dirt. At first it didn't respond, and he thought it might be past saving. But then, after a time, a tiny tremor of sound began in its throat, which rose and fell with the rhythm of his tongue. He did what he could for the purring youngster, marveling at its recuperative powers. At last he sat back, content that it would survive, and tended to his own wounds. He needed to move on now, to figure out how the foul dream-creatures crossed into the waking world. Now that he was aware of both worlds, perhaps he could do that.

He started to leave, then heard a rustling behind him. He looked back and saw that the kitten was on its feet, standing right behind him. Ready to follow. He growled a warning, but the sound lacked sincerity, and—like most kittens—this one ignored adult hostility. With a hiss of exasperation, Hunter-in-Darkness started to move forward again, and to his amazement it trotted along behind him, limping slightly, a brief chirrup indicating that its legs did hurt but yes, it was coming, it would manage to keep up with him somehow.

With a snort of disbelief he began to trot toward his destination. Wondering why he was pleased that the tiny thing—too young to be prudent, too wounded to be helpful—was still alongside him.

* * *

It was there, in the distance. Faint, almost ghostly, its outline uncertain in the shadowland darkness, but clearly there, despite the fact that it shouldn't be visible in the dreamworld.

The white building.

He crept to the edge of the forest, head low, suspicious. The wall between the worlds must be thin indeed, if he could see across it. He looked back to see if the kitten was still beside him. It was. Strangely, that comforted him.

Hovering around the building were many dream-creatures. Malformed ones, even more unwholesome than those which had attacked the kitten. So many of them! They seemed to be waiting for something. But what?

The kitten was the first to move. Too young to be inhibited by fear, it slipped out into the open. Against the short grass its small black form slithered like a snake, bodylight dim. More cautiously, Hunter-in-Darkness followed. He was a larger cat and a brighter one, and the lack of cover made him uneasy; nevertheless he followed, and not until they got to the fence did the two cats stop to consider their situation. The wires were translucent, like the ghost of a fence might be, but that didn't mean its magic was gone. Slowly, prepared for the worst, Hunter-in-Darkness eased one paw forward, and quickly tapped the wire. Human magic guarded this place in the waking lands, but perhaps this ghostly copy might be passable. Indeed, his paw passed through the wires as if smoke; the fence had no solidity in this world, and no power to harm him.

He went through the fence; the kitten followed. A few dream-creatures passed overhead, but they showed no interest in the two cats. They were wholly fixated upon a place just ahead them, where the air was rippling like the surface of a wind-driven lake. One by one they passed through that space, as if through a door. With a quick glance behind him to see if the kitten was still following—it was—Hunter-in-Darkness followed them into the shimmering space.

Entering it was like diving into ice. For an instant he was so cold that he could barely move his body, and he lost all memory of ever having been warm. Panic set in, but he forced himself to keep moving. A moment later the cold and the fear were suddenly gone, and he stumbled out onto a man-made surface, skidding to an undignified halt as he slammed into a wall that had suddenly appeared in front of him.

He was back in the waking world, he realized. And so were the dream-creatures.

He leaped up and grabbed one, and felt his claws tear flesh before he fell back to the floor. Yes! He could hunt them now, in his own world. On his own terms. Then a thudding sound reminded him of his kitten ally, and he turned to find the small cat huddled tail over head at the base of the wall. He pushed it back onto its feet, noting that the impact had reopened a gash along its shoulder. A faint crimson smear marked the spot where it had struck the wall, and it left red footprints as it came to Hunter's side. The larger cat shrugged; there was nothing more he could do for it. But he was relieved that it had managed the crossing safely, and licked the kitten's flank once to welcome it.

A low humming sound could be heard now, coming from down the hallway. Instinctively he knew what it was: the sound of dream-creatures gathering in large numbers. The kitten's ears pricked upright as well, and its tiny tail was fluffed out almost as wide as its body. The sound made Hunter afraid—that, too, was instinctive—but he could not turn back now. He was Hunter-in-Darkness, Crosser-of-Worlds, and this was the enemy he had come to engage.

He followed the sound, and the kitten followed him: down a hallway, through an open doorway, down another hallway, always seeking the source of the sound. His bodylight was bright with anticipation, and the kitten beside him was regaining luminescence with every passing moment. The humming sound was growing louder and louder.

Then he saw the human.

His first reaction was to draw back, hissing. Humans had hurt him badly once, and he had no intention of giving them a chance to do so again. But then he picked up the scent of death from the body. He touched his nose to the cooling flesh, but there was no smell of blood or illness to reveal the cause of death, only the faint residue of dream-creature stink. They must have killed him. And if they could bring down a human of this size, what hope did he, a single cat, have of fighting them?

As if in answer, the kitten chirruped beside him. Two cats, then. It would have to do; cats weren't pack animals by nature, so they had no way of summoning more claws to their aid.

He jumped over the body, not wanting to step on the foul-smelling flesh, and the kitten trotted around it. The sound was so loud now that Hunter-in-Darkness knew they were nearing their destination. They could feel it resonating in their bones, along with a low rumbling sound that reminded Hunter of human tools he had seen in the past. That in turn brought back memories of his kittenhood with sudden clarity. How small the dream-creatures had been back then, how harmless! Without a doubt, they were changing, and whatever was in this white building was responsible.

Then they came to another door, and without hesitation he pushed against it, forcing it to swing open. And at last they had a clear view into the heart of the dream-creature gathering.

There were hundreds of them. Thousands! Small and colorful ones, whose shapes were like those Hunter-in-Darkness had chased in his youth; massive, distorted ones, who flickered in and out of existence as he watched; and some unlike any the cat had ever seen before, with tentacles of black smoke and a smell that made bile rise in the back of his throat. There was another human lying in the far corner, and a dozen of the most distorted dream-creatures were clinging to its body like leeches, feeding on the last of its bodylight.

In the center of the room was a large human-thing: a sleek, rectangular object that vibrated with hunger and death. From its rear end trailed thick black cords, anchoring it to the floor. Many small lights were fixed on its face, and they glittered on and off like a horde of firesprites. Upon a piece of glass at the very top, bright green shapes were visible, words and phrases which no cat or dream-creature could read.

CAUTION

APPLIED TESTS BEGUN 19:53:01

FIRST SEQUENCE IN PROGRESS

DO NOT INTERRUPT

Hunter-in-Darkness had never hated anything before, like he hated that human-thing. But then, he had never killed before, for any reason other than hunger or the pleasure of the hunt. Now the wounded kitten was beside him, and the rage that its plight instilled in him was like fire in his veins. If such deformed creatures were allowed to keep growing, to feed—to *breed*—they would be a threat to both worlds. How long before they began to attack older cats, skilled hunters who were deft with truth and claw, but who couldn't hope to stand up to a pack of this many monsters? How long before cats dared not dream at all, and therefore dared not sleep? No, these creatures must be killed here and now, and Hunter-in-Darkness must do it.

But how? Keeping to the walls, he slowly circled the room, watching them. They hardly seemed to notice him, but focused all their attention on the human-thing in the center of the room. Good. The kitten was still with him, and he was pleased to see that it hadn't given in to its fear. It would make a fine hunter someday, if it survived this confrontation.

Periodically one of the creatures would butt into the human-thing. Trying to hurt it, or move it? Or wanting to get inside? What could be inside that sleek shell, that drew them so? A receptive female, perhaps? Maybe the mother of these creatures? He had to kill whatever was calling to these creatures, he realized. But how?

Suddenly he remembered his own kittenhood, how he had played with his brothers and sisters in the small wooden house, stalking dish towels and fallen pencils and the ultimate great adversary, the black cords. They lay coiled about the base of every magical human-thing, and stretched across the floor like sleeping snakes. Those were humans' most precious possessions, and woe betide the cat who gnawed on them. Dish towels the cats might shred to bits, furniture they might destroy, pencils might be hunted and subdued, but no cat ever dared to touch the black cords. That was absolutely forbidden. One time he had bitten into one before a human managed to stop him, and a jolt of searing pain had thrown him back, even as the human-thing it was attached to went dark. How the humans had yelled at him! The cords were filled with human magic, that much was clear.

Hunter-in-Darkness crouched down against the cold floor, preparing to spring. There was no clear path to the cords; he would have to fight his way through the swarm of dream-creatures to reach them. A flick of his tail kept the tension from freezing his hindquarters as he gauged his distance, then leapt into their midst with all possible force. The creatures were solid to him now, and he slashed out to thrust aside the ones that were between him and his objective. Gore clogged his claws and splattered his fur as he landed some feet short of where he needed to be, hindered by their interference.

They turned on him, then, in numbers too vast to count, armed with teeth and stingers and talons and tentacles and weapons that Hunter-in-Darkness had never seen before. He fought them bravely, gaining ground inch by inch as he did so, but the numbers against him were too overwhelming, and the enemy too well armed. He still could not reach the cords. A paralyzing sting disabled one hind leg, forcing him to drag it behind him. A spiked tail swung directly at his eyes, forcing him backwards a step. Then two. He was losing ground. He would never reach the black cords now, would never be able to attack their magic. He tried to leap forward, desperate to make headway, but he struck a clump of the creatures in mid-air and fell to the floor, stunned. One of the smaller ones sank its twisted fangs into his hind leg. He was losing blood, and could not last much longer.

A screech suddenly split the air, and something that was not a dream-creature bumped into Hunter's hind leg. The fangs which had been fastened to his leg broke loose; foul black blood joined his own on the floor. The kitten had caught up with him, and it shoved him in the flank, urging him with silent insistence: *Go on! Go on!* Another creature attacked Hunter-in-Darkness, but was driven off by the fierce green-eyed kitten. *Go on!* Hunter-in-Darkness dragged himself forward, one rear leg nearly useless now, as the kitten danced around him, screeching its war cry, protecting him from harm. He was close to the magical cords now, and closing in. Only inches left…

His teeth closed about the nearest one, and he pulled back on it, hard. Tearing with his claws at the soft, yielding surface, knowing he must break through quickly or die. His eyes were filled with blood now; he could hardly see, and was maneuvering by feel through a thicket of black cords, clawing in every direction. Tearing at them, wildly. One of them fought back, and it burned him, like the magical fence had once burned him. But the pain only served to increase his determination. He had been right; the magic was *here*.

Now the humming sound was beginning to falter, and the dream-creatures that he could see looked directionless; they were no longer attacking him, but wandered around in random patterns. Good; the kitten might be safe. He slashed at another cord and searing pain lanced through his paw, but the cord seemed to die in consequence, and was safe to touch thereafter. There were very fewcords left intact now; most had lost the magic they needed to hurt him. Besides, there were so few places on him left to be burned...

He slid into the shadowlands, but never knew when. Fell into something that was not quite sleep, but deeper: not quite a dream, but just as compelling.

His last thought was of the kitten.

* * *

The call came at 9:30. By 9:37 Wes was flying out of the house, with Miles in pursuit. Fifteen minutes later they arrived at the facility. There were at least a dozen people gathered around the main entrance to the building, some in police uniforms. He sought out a security guard he knew. "What the hell's going on here?" Wes demanded. "What did Davis mean, a *power failure?* Who are all these people, and what are they doing here?" One woman was in tears, he saw. A policewoman was comforting her.

"This way, sir." The security guard took him firmly by the arm and led him into the building. Not his usual route. That path was blocked by a crowd of guards and medics and the sprawling, lifeless body of a technical assistant from the night shift. Jerry Haskell. "What happened?" Wes demanded.

No one answered.

He almost stopped to demand information. But whatever had happened to Haskell was over and done with; there was nothing Wes could do now to save him. The Eden project, on the other hand, might still be salvaged.

He broke into a run, with no concern for whether Miles could keep up with him. When he reached the door to the computer lab he burst in with a question on his lips, fear like an icy serpent in his heart.

"What the—oh, my God..."

Blood was splattered across one section of the floor, and up and down two sides of the central island. Human blood, or animal? Was that a cat down there, tangled in the smoldering wires? He saw his assistant at the far end of the room, standing with a small small group of guards. Was that Casey's body at their feet? "Davis, what's going on?"

His assistant's expression was grim as he came to join Wes. "Power was interrupted at approximately 8:30. I came to investigate and found...this." He indicated the room, the blood, the body. "I would have called you earlier, but they wanted the police to come in here first."

"That's Casey, isn't it? How did he die?"

Davis shook his head. "No clue. The blood isn't his. They think maybe cardiac arrest. They'll need to do an autopsy to be sure."

Wes looked back at the tangled mess of severed power cords. He could see toothmarks in a few, and one had a disembodied claw stuck in it. What on earth had inspired the cat to attack them like that?

He hesitated, afraid to ask the question that concerned him most. At last he dared it. "How much was lost?"

"Nearly an hour of processing. Data loss depends on whether the power went off cleanly, or there was erratic activity preceding total shutdown. We could be clearing out glitches for days. Rich is online now, trying to save the last test sequence, but that may not be recoverable."

Damn! But it could have been worse. The program would eventually pick up where it had left off, and research would resume. What were the odds, realistically speaking, that the one set of conditions they had been searching for was being tested at the exact moment that the system crashed?

Wes walked over to where the cat's body lay and squatted by its side. Yes, no question about it, this was what had done the damage. Damn the animal! Just like those little nuisances back home, who never knew when to leave things alone.

Then he saw the mark across its forehead, and single white toe on one forward paw, and his face drained of color.

"Dr. McGillis?" It was Davis.

"Go help the medics," he said. He was pleased that his voice sounded steady. "Ask if they need anything."

When his assistant was gone, he whispered to Miles, "Do you recognize it?"

"You mean, does it look like one of your cats? Yes."

He pulled out a pencil and used the point to turn the animal's head to one side. The scar from a bullet wound was clearly visible now, surrounded by streaks of blood and tufts of torn fur. "It's the fourth of that litter,"he whispered. "The one we thought we killed. But how did it survive? My God, the implications …" He reached out a trembling hand to steady himself against the island console. "Fertile, genetically altered, and loose in the woods for months now. Shit. If the feds ever finds out about this, Elsa will lose her license, that's for sure, and as for this project…" He shuddered. "It'll set experimental genetics back a decade if this gets out. All the old fears will rear their ugly heads again. Damn!"

"Do they have to know?" his old friend asked quietly.

Wes looked up at him, a flicker of hope in his eyes. "No. They don't." His grip on the console eased, and slowly he rose to his feet. "They have enough other things to worry about." He looked at Casey's body and his lips tightened. "No one will think to question the cat's genetic background."

And the look in his eyes said it all: *Destroy the cat's body as soon as possible. Lie if necessary. Salvage the program at all costs.*

Wes walked to where Casey's body lay, fielding questions from people as he approached. No, he'd heard nothing about the incident until a mere half hour ago. No, the cat didn't belong to anyone he knew. No, he had no idea how it had gotten in here, or why it had attacked the electrical cords like that.

Miles looked down at the floor again—and then quickly away. No need to say anything about what he saw. Let Wes think, for now, that the trouble was over. He had enough to deal with as it was.

There'd be time enough later, when things had calmed down a bit, for Miles to tell his friend about the kitten tracks.

AUTHOR'S NOTE *for* THE DREAMING KIND

What is it about cats that so fascinates us? On the one hand, they are sweet and fluffy companions who entertain us with their antics and snuggle close on cold nights. On the other hand, they are the breath of the wild come into our homes, ruthless predators that do not abandon their lethal instincts at our threshold. And never is that contrast more evident than during a kitten's 'zoomies': the time when a young cat appears to go insane, and will tear wildly through the house, chasing—and sometimes chased by—imaginary enemies. We watch in fascination as it hisses at empty air, batting at things that do not exist, and wonder what is going in inside its head at that moment. What if the things it is chasing are real? What if it is we humans who do not understand the true nature of the world, because we lack the senses needed to see it clearly?

When Martin Greenberg invited me to submit something to his next anthology, CAT FANTASTIC, it was the first short story that I had ever written without years of background material to draw upon. I regard its creation as a turning point in my life: the day when I became, in my own mind, a professional writer.

THANKSGIVING

I see you walking down the darkened streets
wrapped in a secret, sullen loneliness.
Your footsteps are the only sound for miles,
your phantom thoughts a whisper in the night.
What drives you from the fellowship of man
to these dark places, where no human voice
sings out in fevered pitch the words of thanks
that echo in this season like the wind?
What brings you to this street, where thoughts unwind
in solitude, their secrets undisturbed
by mortal voice, or else immortal guile?
I follow without sound, giving no hint
of my true nature, or of my intent.
As for my hunger, that is best unsaid.
The dead have secrets too.

Hours have passed
since bright-lit windows faded into dark,
since songs gave way to silence, food to dreams,
and prayers of thanks dispersed upon the wind.
What are those things to you? Even the whores
have gone inside tonight. And the drunkards,
bereft of liquor, seek what space they can
to shelter them. The taverns are all closed,
likewise the shops that trade in bottled dreams.
There is no one abroad but you, my friend,
no dream but yours, no need but yours…
…and mine.

I move from out of shadow, so the light
from distant street lamps picks out my features.
I hear you gasp to see my face, this mask,
designed for you, sculpted to suit your need.

I sense your heartbeat quicken – and why not?
I am what you desire me to be,
clothed in that fantasy which is my art,
my sweet seduction born within your soul,
a dream made real. Oh, my lost, lonely one,
did you not know that hunger draws my kind?
As predators are drawn to weakened prey
so am I called to you, your sweet despair
a siren's song no hunter could resist.

I greet you now. Soft sounds, but filled with power.
If I so willed, one word would hold you fast,
or bring you to your knees, where your own hand
would move without volition, cutting flesh,
shedding red blood, warm blood, to suit my need.
But this is not the night for such commands.
It is but hours since this season's theme
resounded in a thousand mortal prayers.
Its echo lingers, softening the night,
blunting the cruel edge of hunger's blade.
So I speak gently, even as my craft
sculpts an illusion that will draw you in.
What is the need that drives you, on this night?
What hunger draws you to this lonely place?
What fantasy do you most wish fulfilled?
I have the power to give you what you want,
and ask in payment... only fair return.

And so I wrap you in my veil, I feed
your heart with visions, and give your soul
one moment's taste of what it most desires.
All in my voice, my eyes, a single glance.
I feel you tremble, and I sense your heart
spurred on to heightened rhythm. Do you dare
invite me home with you, to share these hours
in warmth and privacy, daring to trust,

soul touching soul, cold solitude denied?
The words need not be voiced. I understand.
Who knows loneliness better than my kind?
And so we walk, you with your measured steps,
I with a hunter's pace, silent and cold.
And if someone should hear us, he would say
that but one living creature walked the night.
And judging thus, he would reveal the truth.
But who is listening?

The streets are cold.
I willingly relinquish them for now,
trading the quiet darkness of my realm
for this domain of light and warmth, your own.
Pausing for just a moment at the door,
taking the measure of what lies within:
photographs scattered, bottles spilled, and pain
so poignant I can taste it. Near the door
a picture lies, glass shattered, stained with tears.
Ah, do I look like her? Is she the one?
I wondered whose it was, this face I wore.
And now I see you hesitate, as if
seeing me there beside her is too much.
Your soul is bleeding freshly now, and pain
wells up inside you with hot urgency.
Ah, come into my arms, sweet wounded one,
and drink in the illusion I have made
while I, in turn, drink deeply of your life.
A fair trade, is it not?

Though Death awaits,
I will not give him access to your soul.
Not tonight. Though the hunter in me yearns
for consummation of this killing game
there is another voice inside, gentler,
that speaks in echoes from a distant life

And says no man should die on such a night.
So give yourself into illusion's arms:
one brief embrace, in which to deny truth.
One brief respite, in which to forget pain.
Who gives to whom? And must one ever know?
The question's never answered. Drink your fill.
You cannot kill my kind with loneliness.
And I, though death looms dark at each embrace,
will not let hunger sever life's last tie,
not on this night, when mortal grace holds sway.
So do not fear this feasting, nor its price.
This predator remembers mortal days.
And though the years have dimmed my human view
I recall gratitude, remember prayers,
and in my unliving, unbeating heart,
I, too, give thanks.

AUTHOR'S NOTE *for* THANKSGIVING

I'm not quite sure what inspired me to experiment with combining urban fantasy and Shakespearean iambic pentameter, but I was pleased with how it came out.

PANDORA

On Monday of week 213, McKellan's appendix burst. Until that moment I hadn't even realized he still had an appendix, and I must shamefully admit that I was so surprised that I wasn't much help. After the others carried him off to the med lab and adjusted the ship's spin for surgery-friendly gravity, I checked the regulations in our archives. I discovered that while it wasn't strictly required for crew members to have their appendixes removed before launch—as it was for tonsils, and several other bits of vestigial flesh that had a reputation for causing issues—it was strongly encouraged. Logic certainly suggested that if you were going to spend eleven years in space with limited medical facilities, you might want to get rid of everything that could cause you trouble along the way, right? But some people didn't like the thought of being carved up like a piece of meat, even if it was the rational thing to do.

Go figure.

The surgery itself wasn't a big deal—roboticized laparoscopy—but Captain Basinger gave him a dressing-down afterwards that probably hurt like hell. She was spending her most fertile years in space with her tubes tied, she reminded him, and if she could give up the very core of her fecundity and womanhood for the sake of our mission, he should damn well be willing to remove an organ that had passed its evolutionary expiration date.

And with that for a eulogy, McKellan's appendix went the way of all other biological material on the Ponce de Leon, cleansed and sterilized and broken down to its base components so it could serve as raw material for fuel, clothing, or breakfast bars. Waste not, want not.

Later I asked McKellan why he had made the choice he did, back on Earth, and he told me that at the time he had believed the human body was a sacred thing, and you shouldn't remove any parts of it unless you absolutely had to. That really surprised me. The traditional qualifications for a Bellasi mission were a list of minimalisms: low sex drive, low political passion, low religious commitment…low anything that might cause human conflict when you were sealed in a small container with seven other people for the better part of eleven years. I did a two-year mission once, and trust me, the smallest interpersonal tensions could evolve into raging emotional firestorms when people were trapped together for that long. Hence the reason the folks on the first Mars expedition needed so much therapy after they came home, with one of them committing suicide later. If McKellan had told our vetting officers that religious beliefs prevented him from agreeing to a basic safety precaution, he'd have been dumped from the mission before he could draw breath to say another sentence.

But that was water under the bridge now. Soon the captain's ire would be water under the bridge as well. You only had two choices on a mission like ours: learn to let go of things, or go crazy. Thus far, no one had chosen to go crazy.

McKellan was an atheist now. Which was not as odd as it might sound. Out here in the vast emptiness of interstellar space, cut off from the planet that was humanity's spiritual center, some people found God. Others lost sight of Him.

It was all in the handbook.

* * *

Ten thousand years ago, the human race was huddling for warmth on an ice-sheathed planet, fashioning crude knives and arrows from chips of stone, wondering where all the nice meaty mammoths had gone.

Ten thousand years ago, an alien race was colonizing the far reaches of the galaxy, harvesting energy from the stars, living in harmony with nature and with themselves. They had no poverty. They had no war. They had evolved past the need for societal suffering, and they spread across the galaxy peacefully, optimistically, establishing cities that were sleek, clean, and self-maintaining. If they happened across a planet that was already inhabited by intelligent beings they didn't try to conquer it, or steal its resources, or interfere with it in any way. They just left it alone to decide its own fate, and if and when it reached the stars, the aliens welcomed it as an equal, sharing the knowledge that would allow it to rise above its own primitive origins and become part of the galactic community.

We named them the Bellasi because we didn't know what they called themselves. It seemed appropriate: The Beautiful Ones.

Five thousand years ago, humankind raised pyramids on the shores of the Nile, built storehouses of grain to guard against famine, and learned how to write, forge metal, and brew beer. Millennia would pass before the first men would break free of Earth's grip and travel to the stars, but already they were mapping the heavens, paving the way. Meanwhile there were wars to fight, wealth to hoard, people to oppress, territory to conquer. Traditional human passtimes.

Five thousand years ago, the Bellasi vanished. Their gleaming cities were left empty on a thousand worlds, inhabitants gone without a trace. All that the Beautiful Ones had accomplished—all that they had dreamed of—disappeared into the galactic darkness without a ripple. And the many races that had gathered beneath their banner followed them into oblivion. As they had shared in the Bellasi's prosperity, so they shared in their fate. All gone.

No one knew why.

* * *

I was eight years old when our scouts returned home with news of an alien city they had discovered. Our school held a grand assembly to celebrate the event, twelve hundred students crowded into a humid auditorium to watch the 3-D images as they streamed in: the first alien civilization ever discovered. How sleek their buildings seemed, how graceful, how eerily empty! Even as children we could sense the wrongness of it, and we yearned for something to explain that emptiness. We longed to see half-eaten food on a table, that would hint at a hasty exit. Clothing strewn across the floor, from when they had packed to escape some disaster. Even bodies struck down by a rogue bacteria, War-of-the-Worlds style, would have at least given us a story we could understand. But the aliens had left their city in perfect order, with no sign of foul play or urgency. The ultimate mystery.

More and more cities were discovered after that, always empty. Sometimes we found images of the Bellasi themselves, featured in relief carvings that revealed their history. From these we learned that they had welcomed other species into the galactic community by sharing the knowledge that allowed them to transcend their primitive instincts and create an enlightened society. This was first done on the Bellasi homeworld, later on their colony planets, in ritual chambers designed for that purpose. We learned that they had developed technology that could transfer knowledge directly from one mind to another (and later we found a few recorded messages that were still active, so we could experience this for ourselves). And we found images of a box-shaped object covered in strange designs, which supposedly contained the device the Bellasi used to share the secret of their enlightenment with other species. The device itself was never depicted.

Some called it a delusion, a Bellasi legend. Others called it a God Box. Scientists called it a Neurological Transfer Interface and they wrote long and elegant papers speculating about its nature. Perhaps it would reveal a secret technology to make clean, low-cost energy universally available. Or a method of conditioning that could transform a species' violent and primitive urges into a more civilized attitude. Or a religious revelation so profound that it altered the very nature of the soul.

Some called it the Holy Grail.

Our job was to find it.

* * *

"It's out there," Vince Caswell muttered for the fiftieth time that day. "I know it's out there!"

He had his charts displayed on every screen of the control room, preempting our normal visuals. To me they looked like the scribblings of a deranged child, but he kept insisting they were star charts, so okay, call them star charts. To be fair, his calculations had helped us locate more than a dozen Bellasi worlds, so it was hard to argue about his methods. Then again, the Bellasi had colonized every human-inhabitable planet in this part of the galaxy, so their cities weren't exactly hard to find.

He claimed to have an algorithm that could lead us to the Bellasi homeworld, provided we collected enough data to run it. Our mission was to visit colony after colony, so he could take measurements and shoot pictures and scrape paint samples from buildings, or whatever he needed to feed the monstrous appetite of that algorithm. In theory, he was examining subtle trends in Bellasi architecture so that he could extrapolate backwards to their source, but since all Bellasi cities looked the same to me, I was more than a little skeptical. Then again, what did I know about groundbreaking anthropological algorithms? I was just the guy who fixed solar collectors and fine-tuned the waste management system. Handyman in space.

"You see?" he said excitedly, pointing to one of the displays. "There! There! That's where the proportional shift started. I knew I would find it!"

Of course I didn't see it. In the same way that there were wavelengths of light that your average human being couldn't detect, there were aspects of Vince's genius that were invisible to the rest of us. In truth, I would have been happy to do my job and leave him alone to do his, but he needed everyone to be as excited about his work as he was, so he kept trying to explain it to us. Over and over and over again. And yeah, sometimes we pretended that we understood more than we did. It made him feel appreciated, and it cut down on the number of repetitions. Win-win.

"We need to go here next," he said, and he pointed to a region of space that was far, far away from our current location. I sighed. Transportation was something I understood. Inspecting the jump engines so that we didn't wind up stranded between *here* and *there* while the space-time continuum convulsed around us, I also understood. That didn't mean I liked it.

* * *

I hate jumpsleep. Yes, I understand why it's necessary. When you fold space-time into infinite layers and shove a ship through the middle of them, the human mind just doesn't deal with that well. Even rats go bonkers afterwards, running in circles and chewing their own tails off. And natural sleep isn't good enough to protect you. The parts of your brain that handle reason and impulse control have to be shut down completely if they're going to survive the journey. Which means you have to submit to an artificial coma: induced, controlled, and ultimately terminated by machines whose priority is your survival, not your comfort.

The problem is that it's not a natural state, but a soul-sucking unconsciousness akin to death. You panic instinctively as you sense it approach, but your motor control centers have been shut down for the duration, so you can't move at all. Which causes you to panic even more, of course. And as the thick, suffocating blackness closes in around you, you imagine you can feel your brain dissolving cell by cell, your consciousness erased thought by thought, your soul obliterated from reality.

Someday they'll come up with a tranquilizer that's compatible with the process. Probably after I've retired.

* * *

The first time I set foot on a Bellasi world I was only twenty-three. I'll never forget the moment the lander hatch opened and I stepped out into the heart of that glorious, star-shaped city. Granted, the buildings weren't quite as sleek as I had expected them to be. Solar-powered bots kept the streets clean and repaired any major damage, but they could not erase the feeling of age that clung to everything. But still. I was standing in the middle of an alien city.

How cool was that?

Because it was my first Bellasi experience, the crew let me wander around a bit and explore. I found apartments the Bellasi had lived in, and everything inside them was neatly arranged, as if the owners might return at any moment. Had there been bodies here once, that the ubiquitous cleaning bots had cleared away? Or had it always looked like this? I found a garden of glittering solar collectors whose panels shifted to follow the sunlight; when a cloud cast a shadow over them they rippled like a field of agitated butterflies. Eerie and beautiful.

Eventually we headed to the center of the city to find the Bellasi welcoming chamber. It was a vast domed space, much bigger than I'd expected; ten thousand people could have gathered in it without feeling crowded. In the center was a circle of stone statues, some depicting Bellasi, others alien species. They all faced the center of the circle, where a pedestal stood. According to the historical murals, the artifact we sought should be sitting on top of that.

But it wasn't.

I visited dozens of Bellasi worlds after that. Each star-shaped city looked the same. Each had a ritual chamber in its center. A circle of statues was always present, though the alien species that were depicted might vary.

The pedestal was always empty.

* * *

"Hey, Mike, there's something you need to see."

I looked up from the air filtration panel I was trying to repair and saw Kristen Belle, our med tech. "Bit busy at the moment," I told her.

"No, you're not." She took the panel out of my hand and put it aside. "Trust me."

I tried to get her to tell me what was up, but she just smiled enigmatically and gestured for me to follow her. Since it was clearly the only way I was going to get any answers, I did so.

Everyone else was already in the control room when we arrived, staring at something on the main screen. A couple of people nodded a greeting as we entered, but no one turned to look at us. It was as if their eyes were glued to the screen. My heart skipped a beat as I joined them. I was trying not to jump to any conclusions, but this far out in the galaxy, how many things were there to stare at?

On the screen was a planet, displayed in several magnifications. A global view was in the upper left corner, and at first glance I thought it was another Bellasi colony. The typical star-shaped city peeked between cloud banks, immense enough to be visible from space. That was pretty normal. But the arms of the star weren't perfectly even, and one of them wasn't even straight. That was odd. The Bellasi loved regularity.

Then I looked at the close-up views, and I understood why.

Every inch of the planet had been developed, but without any sense of a master plan. I saw primitive construction in some places—brick and mortar, concrete and glass—and high-tech synthetics in others. Even the star city had a sense of chaos about it, different parts constructed out of different materials, in different styles. That wasn't what a Bellasi colony city should look like, I thought. But it was what a planet might look like if a species had evolved there, each new generation layering its construction over what had been built before.

"Welcome to the Bellasi homeworld," Caswell announced.

"Holy shit," I whispered.

We'd found it. We'd really found it! I stared at the screen in disbelief, half expecting the planet to disappear when I blinked. But it didn't. Caswell's damned algorithm had worked! And if his other theories were equally valid, then the Bellasi interface must be down there somewhere. Earth's salvation was at hand, and we were the ones who would deliver it.

To say that we were jubilant would be an understatement. Basinger broke out her private store of quality scotch, and we laughed and we drank and we danced and some of us even cried, caught up in an elation as complex as it was intense. We were crusaders entering Jerusalem, Columbus sighting land, soldiers raising the flag on Iwo Jima, marathon runners crossing the finish line with arms raised, the blood-red ribbon cutting across our chests as a thousand spectators screamed our names. We were all the dreams of Earth. We were all the hungers of mankind. Manifest. Satisfied. Transcended.

Thus do gods celebrate.

* * *

As we approached the Bellasi homeworld, we sent out messages. We filled the darkness of space with our humble attempts at saying hello, and then waited breathlessly for a response. Any kind of response. Because if there was a single Bellasi left alive in the galaxy, surely this was where he would be.

But there was only silence.

On Sunday of week 233 we established orbit around the planet, and we took two landers down to the center of the star-shaped city. That was where the ritual chamber had been located on all the colony planets, so we figured it would be there on this planet as well. But it wasn't. We searched in expanding circles from the central point, inspecting the nearest buildings room by room, looking for any clue as to where a facility like that might be located.

We found nothing.

All of us were suffering from frayed nerves at that point. To come this close to realizing Earth's greatest dream, and not be able to close the deal, was frustrating for all of us. For Caswell it was infuriating. He rushed from building to building like a man possessed, and each time his search came up empty he would curse the planet, or the Bellasi, or even God, like this was some kind of personal affront. It wasn't helping my state of mind, so when Basinger asked for a volunteer to take a lander up and get a bird's-eye view of the city, I jumped at the chance.

Peace at last.

But no matter how long I stared at the city from overhead, I couldn't find any clue to help direct us in our search. Wherever the ritual chamber was—if it was on this planet at all—it was well hidden. Finally, with a sigh, I reported my findings to Captain Basinger. I could hear the frustration in her voice as she thanked me for trying, and somewhere in the background Caswell started cursing.

I didn't feel up to dealing with him, so I asked if I could stay up a bit longer.

Staring down at the city—sensing the vastness of the planet beyond it—I suddenly wondered if our search had been doomed from the start. What if we were looking in the wrong place? Yes, this star city looked like all the others, but in fact it was nothing like them. The others had been planned out completely before the first shovelful of dirt was moved; nothing was left to chance. This city had grown organically, possibly over the course of centuries. And while it might be the biggest and most dramatic city on the planet, visible from space, that didn't mean it was the most significant location to the Bellasi.

So what kind of place would be?

I asked if I could take the lander out further, to explore the surrounding terrain. Just a hunch, I told Captain Basinger. Since no one had any better ideas, she said yes.

And so I left the star-shaped city behind. Maybe I would be able to find the Holy Grail on my own, maybe not. But the peace of solitary flight was soothing, and I wasn't ready to give it up just yet.

* * *

I flew low over the main continent, across a narrow sea, past a few volcanic islands, to the second largest land mass. As I did so, images from the planet's surface scrolled across my screen. I saw gleaming metropolises surrounded by simpler towns, and ancient monuments whose original purpose had probably been forgotten long before the Bellasi discovered space travel. It made the aliens seem more human to me. No longer were they cartoon caricatures of peace and perfection, but flawed beings who had evolved from primitive roots just like we had, each generation building upon lessons learned from the last.

Where would such a species choose to house their most precious artifact? On the colony planets the Bellasi had no choice about the matter: everything in the star-shaped cities was equally new, equally planned, and no one location had any more cultural significance than any other. But here, on a world that was rich with historical resonance, there might be better options. Maybe the Bellasi would want a setting with sacred overtones, something linked to the founding of their civilization.

I had the lander's computer scan all available data, searching for locations that might fit the bill. Alas, there were too many to count, and without better knowledge of Bellasi history, I had no way to narrow the options down. I tapped an agitated finger on the control panel as I tried to come up with some detail that would distinguish my target site from all the others, some single feature that would tell me which location the Bellasi had favored....

And then it hit me.

Trembling with excitement, I had the computer identify any site that had multiple launch facilities nearby. Because if the Bellasi transfer ritual was performed there, surely visitors from other worlds would want to attend. There would be hordes of them, all arriving at the same time, all needing places to land and store their spacecraft, places to eat and rest and entertain themselves in their spare time, as well as easy transportation to and from the ritual site. In the great star cities, arrangements like that were common; those vast metropolises had been built to accommodate interplanetary activity. But an older site would not have had those conveniences. Its location would have been chosen for historical resonance, not architectural convenience, and the launch pads would have to be built wherever space could be found, perhaps linked to the ritual location by roads that twisted through ancient villages. High tech and ancient history intermingled, in that wonderful, uncomfortable way that Earth was so familiar with.

How many sites like that could there be?

The computer found three. One was in a sandstone desert, a meteor strike pit with twisted, wind-carved monuments arranged around the rim. Since there was no building nearby large enough to accommodate the crowds that would have attended the transfer ritual, I ruled that one out. The second was an island with a forest of primitive statues, connected to other islands by a spiderweb of roads. Again, I saw no place there where a great number of people could gather, so, two down. The third was an ancient columned temple, like the Parthenon in style but ten times larger, atop a windswept hill. The roads leading out from it had a vaguely star-shaped plan, as if the Bellasi had tried to apply the same template they used in their colonies, but the terrain had prevented them from doing so perfectly. At the end of each road was a launch facility surrounded by modern buildings. Enough to house thousands.

My heart began to pound as pictures of the place scrolled before me. *This is it*, I thought. *I've found it.* Trembling, I reached for the com to call Captain Basinger and the others; surely it was my duty to let them share in this amazing moment! But what if I was wrong? Having them fly two hours to get here, their hearts filled with hope, only to face another disappointment, wasn't going to improve the spirit of the mission. I owed it to them to at least do a basic recon, and confirm that the site was worth investigating further.

I ordered the lander to set me down just outside the temple building. The air when I disembarked was hot and dry, and for a moment I just stood there, breathing it in, trying to steel my nerves for what might turn out to be the galaxy's greatest disappointment. Then I started walking through the field of dry scrub that surrounded the building. From the condition of the place I guessed there were no maintenance bots active, though I did find the rusted remnants of one. The building's façade was pitted and cracked and there were places where whole sections had come loose, so that the ground was littered with debris. I picked my way over some sharp gravel to get to what remained of the door, two stubs of rotted wood hanging loosely from verdigris hinges. Beyond them was a chamber that was cavernous, dark, and still. The place had an eerie quality to it, like it wasn't so much *empty* as *waiting*. I turned on my shoulder lamp as I entered, looking warily around me for signs of lurking wildlife; the place would be a perfect lair for some large animal. But nothing was moving. Nothing made a sound. Nothing was visible near the door except a scattering of leaves that the wind had blown in.

Then my light crossed the center of the room, and my heart stopped for a moment.

Time itself seemed to stop.

It was there. The same circle of statues we had seen on a dozen other worlds. Only this time all of the figures were Bellasi, and they were carved from a translucent white stone that glowed when my light hit it, giving them the aspect of angels. In the center of the circle was the same kind of pedestal we had seen on so many worlds, only this time it wasn't bare. This time there was something on top of it, a bronze-colored box with alien symbols all over it. Could this really be the technology Earth had sought for so long? Was I really going to go down in history as the man who found it?

Slowly I walked towards it. There were strips of gold metal wrapped around the box, like ribbons on a Christmas present, and they were fastened at the top with a faceted glass ball that I recognized as a message conveyer. My throat was so dry I could barely swallow. How long had it been since anyone had been here? When had the last Bellasi died, leaving their most precious artifact unattended? I'd never been much on religion, but it was hard to believe I would be facing this moment if someone or something hadn't guided me here.

Call the others. The thought seemed distant, unreal. I was in a world of my own now, and my hand slowly moved toward the crystal as if of its own accord. How could you look at such a thing and not want to touch it? *There's nothing to be afraid of,* I told myself. *The crystal is just a message carrier. The thing that has the power to change worlds is inside that box.*

My fingers made contact with the crystal. It was colder than the room at first, but warmed to a fiery heat as my touch activated it.

I saw the Bellasi.

There were dozens of them in the chamber, with skin tones ranging from bleached marble to polished ebony. I saw adult males and females in equal number—no children—and they were closing in on the box with crude weapons in hand: heavy axes, massive wooden clubs, the kinds of tools that one would normally not associate with a high-tech empire. Then a tall male stepped in front of the artifact, protecting it with his body as he tried to get them to back away. As he gestured around the room, I saw the shattered remnants of similar boxes littering the floor, and I understood that this was the last one of its kind. Finally he got the mob to back off. He sighed deeply, then placed a crystal upon the box: the same one I was now touching. This message was from him.

A quick succession of visions unfolded in my mind. I saw the Bellasi as they had been eons before, when their homeworld still teemed with life: a creative, passionate, restless people. I saw magnificent art being produced—paintings crafted in colors I couldn't name, alien symphonies so beautiful that they would have made Beethoven weep. I watched as new generations were born, each child striving to surpass its parents. And I sensed in them the same hunger that had driven my species to explore the stars. I knew that despite their alien appearance, they were human in every way that mattered.

The visions started to come more quickly after that. I saw the Bellasi empire at its peak, star-shaped cities gleaming in the interstellar darkness, spaceships dancing around them like drunken moths. There were other sentient species, some of them human in form and others so alien I couldn't tell which end was which, all living in harmony with each other. No one seemed to have greater duty than to seek his own vision of happiness, for the gross physical requirements of life were all managed by machines, and the great cities were self-sustaining. It was everything Earth dreamed of, and more.

Yet it all seemed wrong to me. I didn't know why. I kept staring at the images, wondering what it was about them that made my skin crawl, what wrongness I sensed in them, just below the level of conscious awareness, that made me so terribly afraid.

And then I realized what it was.

The children were gone.

There had been many of them in the beginning, I was sure of that. I remembered seeing large families in the parks, gathering beneath the glittering solar-collection trees to laugh and play. But there were fewer and fewer children as the visions progressed, each generation becoming smaller than the last. And now this. When had the point of no return been reached? Had some Bellasi seen the end coming, and tried to convince the inhabitants of Paradise that devoting years to nurturing and training and disciplining a child would be more appealing than a life of easy contentment? If so, the effort had failed. The Bellasi had created a world in which challenges were not viewed as a source of inspiration, but as hardships to be eradicated. And what greater challenge was there than to bring a new life into the world? Now, in this glittering galactic empire, there were no children at all, even among the alien species. I was looking at the last generation of Bellasi, the ones who would leave behind empty cities for us to find.

The final vision faded, and I saw the male Bellasi again. This time he seemed to be looking directly at me, and though I knew that it was only a vision, and the being who had crafted it was not actually present, the effect was unnerving. *Now you know.* He was speaking in a language I didn't understand, but the Bellasi technology allowed me to grasp his meaning. *You must choose your own course.* A terrible sadness filled his eyes. *I am sorry.*

The vision disappeared.

I stood there in shock, trying to make sense of what I had just seen. Had Bellasi life truly become so effortless that the labor and sacrifice necessary to raise a child were deemed too great a burden? Or was the reason for their demise more primal than that? Was the struggle for survival so hard-wired into Bellasi genes that once it was gone there was nothing left to drive them? I remembered the magnificent art of their early period, and compared it to the bland, sterile cities in my later visions. It was not only the children that had disappeared, I realized. Without challenges to meet, without obstacles to overcome, the spirit of their race had been wasting away for centuries. And all the species that had joined them in Paradise, embracing the dream of easy prosperity, had followed them into oblivion. Killed by contentment.

In the end the Bellasi had recognized their mistake; that was the meaning of my first vision. They had started to destroy all copies of the Interface, to keep other species from suffering their fate. But the guiding philosophy of their civilization prohibited them from dictating to other species what they must do, and so in the end they had left one intact, perhaps as a sign of respect for the autonomy of sentient beings. Or perhaps as a test.

You must choose your own course, the Bellasi had said.

I was shivering now, and not just from physical cold. The burden of destiny that had fallen upon the Ponce de Leon's crew seemed greater than any human company could bear. Because if we came home with the interface, there was no question what would happen. Philosophers might argue about the wisdom of embracing Bellasi technology, but in the end someone would activate the thing. No one would dare forbid it. The eight of us must decide, right here and right now, if we were willing to deliver to Earth the seeds of its own destruction.

No, I thought suddenly. *Not the eight of us.*

Caswell would never agree to keep our discovery a secret; too much of his ego was invested in this mission. And I didn't think Captain Basinger would go for it, either. She had sacrificed too much to come out here, and returning home without the artifact would make it all meaningless.

If I brought the artifact back to the ship, it would be delivered to Earth. And if it was delivered to Earth, it would be activated.

The choice was mine to make, and mine alone.

My legs started shaking so badly I feared they wouldn't support me; weakly I lowered myself to my knees before the pedestal, while the stone angels looked on in silence. I wasn't the one who should be deciding this. No single person should have the fate of his entire people placed upon his shoulders, least of all someone who was trained to fix broken waste disposal units, not solve existential dilemmas.

In my mind's eye I saw all the miseries of earth laid out before me. Poverty and war, hunger and injustice, an endless tide of suffering that man had struggled against for all his existence. The Bellasi interface could free Earth from all that, forever. If I denied Earth access to their knowledge, then all future suffering would be on my head. Millions upon millions of people, down through the ages, would suffer because of me. It was a magnitude of guilt the human mind could barely grasp.

But if I delivered the Interface, what then? Mankind might enjoy unparalleled peace and prosperity, but for how long? A thousand years, ten thousand? In my mind's eye I saw the millions of people who would never be born if the Bellasi interface was activated. Countless human lives that might have been filled with art and beauty and passion and hope as well as pain, now would never exist. Because of me.

"Don't make me choose," I whispered. But who was I pleading

with—the same God who had brought me here? If He existed, then He was a merciless bastard, for placing this decision in my hands.

My com buzzed. It was Captain Basinger, wanting a report on my progress. Numbly I told her I was about to head back to base camp, and I would give her a full report when I arrived. That left me about two hours to decide which course of action was the right one. But deep in my heart I knew that both were right, and neither was right. Whichever one I chose would leave me haunted by ghosts forever.

I thought about the Bellasi colonies we'd visited: serene, but oh so sterile. Long before the Bellasi had died out they had lost the spark that earned them the stars in the first place. Was that what would happen to humanity, as well? Would the price of Bellasi contentment be the loss of all that made us human? That was a kind of death, wasn't it?

Slowly I rose to my feet, walked to the pedestal, and stared at the Interface. Then I reached out and picked it up. It was surprisingly light, for something so philosophically weighty. I brought it back to my lander and put it on the seat beside me. Trying not to look at it. Trying not to think.

Sometimes it's not a question of what the right choice is, so much as what choice we think we can live with.

* * *

Maybe I should have thrown it into a volcano, Frodo-style, so that it was destroyed forever. Maybe the deep sea crevasse that I dropped it into won't be enough to guard it from those who, if they learned it was there, would empty the oceans of this world with a teaspoon if they had to, to retrieve it.

People will keep looking for it, of course. Caswell has already come up with a theory about why the Bellasi homeworld was never the right location for our search, and he's fine tuning his algorithms so we'll know where to look next. No one's questioning him about it. We all understand how important it is for people to believe that the Interface is still out there somewhere, a magical solution to all of our ills, just over the next horizon. Even if we told people it didn't exist, no one would believe us. And so we keep searching.

Maybe an ancient knight did find the Holy Grail one day. Maybe he held it in his hand, awed by its holiness, but then God sent him a vision of what human society would become if he brought it home. And he wound up leaving it behind. Or hiding it away. Or even destroying it. Because he realized that sometimes wanting a thing is better for the human soul than actually having it.

I named the planet Pandora. The others argued in favor of names they liked better, but we had agreed long ago that we would take turns naming the planets we found, and this time, by chance, the choice fell to me. So Pandora it was.

Next Sunday we go back into jumpsleep. Black, dreamless, obliterating.

I'm looking forward to it.

AUTHOR'S NOTE for PANDORA

When Joshua Palmatier invited me to submit a story to his upcoming anthology, ALIEN ARTIFACTS, I had just been reading about declining birth rates in developed countries. They have been below replacement level (2.1 children per couple) for some time now, and in some countries are as low as 1.3. A nation whose people do not reproduce cannot sustain itself. But why is it happening? Studies suggest that the more educated people are, the fewer children they tend to have. High-income earners also tend to have fewer children, and to have them later in life. In short, those who are wealthy and educated often want to focus on launching their careers--and enjoying the fruits of those careers--without taking time out to focus on the time-consuming demands of raising a child.

Those were the thoughts going through my mind when I wrote "Pandora", which explores one possible consequence of such a trend.

BAD TRIP
AUTHOR'S NOTE

For this next story, I am putting the note at the beginning to provide context.

In 2010, I volunteered to teach a writing workshop at a juvenile detention facility in California. The teens there were excited to have a break from their normal routine, and they participated enthusiastically. For my last presentation, I offered them a challenge: they could give me any story elements they wanted—character, setting, plotline—and no matter how crazy or disconnected those elements seemed, I would make a cohesive story out of them. My intention was to show them that a creative mind could weave stories out of just about anything.

Well, I had forgotten where I was. After an energetic group argument about what elements to require, I was given the following:1) The main character is a meth junkie. 2) He is chosen as First Contact for aliens visiting Earth. 3) Because they want meth. 4) He either prevents or causes an alien invasion (my choice)

This is what I wrote for them.

Louie cursed on his way up the staircase. By itself that was not a
noteworthy event; his neighbors had long since resigned themselves
to the stream of profanity that accompanied his exit from the
building, as well as the matching one that heralded his homecoming.
But today's tirade was of a higher volume and sharper quality than
usual, and was accompanied by a series of loud thumps as his fist
struck the grimy wall of the stairwell. Apparently in his meth-induced
haze he believed that he could drive his hand through solid concrete.

No one got in his way. You didn't mess with Louie when he was
high. Which generally meant that you didn't mess with Louie at all.

He fumbled for the keys to his small apartment, staggered inside,
and slammed the door shut behind him. "FUCK!" The expletive
reverberated throughout the dimly lit apartment, the peeling walls
echoing his frustration and rage back at him. "FUCK FUCK FUCK!"
He picked up some unnamed object and hurled it at the far wall in
rage, hoping for a satisfying spectacle of destruction, but he had long
ago stopped leaving breakable items near the door. The object made
an unsatisfying thud as it added a new dent to the drywall, and then it
fell to the floor, bouncing twice before it rolled to a stop right near his
feet. He kicked it away with a growl.

He had lost three customers today. Big customers. Two of them
had been picked up by the police while on the streets, but the third
had been nabbed in a raid at the club just as Louie was showing up to
make a delivery. He'd almost gotten caught up in the raid himself,
and only a quick exit through the bathroom window and an hour of
cowering deep in the club's dumpster had spared him the
awkwardness of having to explain to the cops why he had half a
dozen packets of meth hidden in the lining of his jacket. Like there
was anything good you could say about that.

What a fucking rotten day.

His jacket smelled of rotten garbage now—no big surprise—so he
pulled it off and dropped it in a heap by the door. He was too agitated
to sit down, so he paced back and forth nervously, striding from the
foldout couch that he never bothered opening to the dingy refrigerator
that he never bothered stocking in five quick steps. It was a tiny
studio apartment, but it kept the rain off his head and gave him a safe

place to stash his drugs. What man needed more than that?

A cold wind whistled in through the frame of the apartment's one window, raising goosebumps along his neck. The heat in the apartment had been shut off last month, along with all the other utilities, and while he'd managed to get the lights back on and the toilet running, central heating was a luxury he still couldn't afford. He kicked the kerosene space heater in frustration as he passed, as if hoping it would just light itself in self-defense, but the small part of his brain that was still capable of rational thought knew that he'd have to feed it some more fuel before it could function. And with only half a can of kerosene in the house (*Do Not Store Kerosene In This Container!* it said), he wasn't going to do that until it got really cold.

He picked up a grimy glass from the counter and was about to pour himself a drink of water when the refrigerator began to glow. Hurriedly he dropped the glass and backed away, trying not to knock over the can of kerosene in his retreat.

The light rapidly became so bright that he had to shield his eyes. From what little he could make out it didn't seem to be coming from the refrigerator itself, so much as the space that surrounded it. When he had backed up all the way to the front door he knelt down and fumbled for his jacket—though whether that was because he wanted the small handgun in its pocket or because in times of stress his first instinct was to protect his product, he could not say.

The light was as bright as a thousand naked light bulbs, and when he shut his eyes to protect them it burned right through his eyelids. Then, just when he started seeing spots swimming in front of him, it receded. As his eyes readjusted, he could make out a rectangular frame where the refrigerator used to be, like an oversized doorway without a wall attached. While he stood there gaping at it, a giant lizard stepped through.

Now he was sure it was the gun he wanted.

It was sleek and black and it stood on its hind legs like that lizard in those insurance commercials, its crested head brushing the ceiling. One swipe of its long, muscular tail would have trashed everything in the apartment. Its neck was covered with iridescent frills that fluttered with each breath. A thin black tube came out of the corner of its mouth and ran down its neck to some kind of collar, and a faint acrid odor seemed to emanate from its skin. Acetone?

Louie pulled out his gun and fired at the thing, his hand shaking as he pulled the trigger again and again and again, until he ran out of ammunition. Most of the bullets hit the wall surrounding his target, but in an apartment this small even a meth-addled junkie could not miss every shot. Two bullets hit the creature head-on, and bounced off its sleek scaly hide like they were made of rubber.

Bounced off.

"Fuck," he whispered hoarsely.

The lizard blinked once, then fiddled with a small black apparatus that was strapped to its chest. After a moment it hissed into the object and a rasping mechanical voice came out of it. "Is this good? Is this your language? I do not have 'fuck' in my linguistic databank."

The fact that the thing seemed to be speaking with an Australian accent only made the whole scene more bizarre. "Where did you come from?" Louie rasped. "Why are you here? Are you going to kill me?"

The giant lizard was silent for a moment, evidently listening to the strange sounds that were emanating from its translator. Finally it began to hiss again. "To kill you? No. I have come...how do you say? In peace. Yes, that is it. I-have-come-in-peace."

It all would have been hard enough to absorb on a good day, and this was not a good day. "Why come here?" Louie demanded. "Don't you want the leader of Earth or something like that? I'm no one important."

"I have come to buy meth," the lizard said. "You sell meth, that is correct? I have come to achieve a purchase."

Louie blinked. "Say what?"

"I have come to buy meth," it repeated. "I have access to many things that you value. Our trading will be an act of mutual happiness."

Yeah, Louie thought derisively. *Right. A giant reptile has come all the way across the fucking universe just to purchase drugs from me. Cause I'm the best fucking drug dealer in the whole fucking galaxy, right? Tell me another one.*

But then, with a sinking feeling in his gut, he realized what must really be going on. Earth was probably on the brink of some kind of alien invasion. This creature had come to see if humans were strong enough to stand up to his people, or if they would make useful slaves, or something like that. Louie didn't have a clue why an alien lizard would start off its campaign in his apartment in particular, but maybe that had to do with somebody who had lived here before him. Maybe the CIA had set up shop here once, and left something important behind, that the aliens wanted. That would explain the listening devices he sometimes saw the cockroaches whispering into.

"I haven't got any meth," he told it, trying to sound braver than he felt. "So you can go away now, back to your Lizardopolis or wherever you came from. Okay? No meth here."

The lizard cocked its head. "Detector says meth is present. Detector says…" He pointed. "There."

The black, scaly finger was pointing to the wall behind Louie's unused oven, the very spot where he hid his main stash. A chill ran up his spine. Whatever drug-locating technology these guys had, he was sure glad the cops on Earth didn't know about it.

Then he realized: *He's here to raid my stash.*

Now he was really angry. The thought of aliens conquering Earth was bad enough. But the thought of this giant lizard stealing his drugs...that was personal.

"I will pay you well," the lizard persisted. "I have many trade goods of different types. Reveal what you value."

Drawing in a deep breath, Louie forced himself to nod. In his current state it was hard for him to organize enough brain cells to come up with a meaningful plan, but a few useful thoughts flickered weakly inside his skull. He made a show of putting his empty gun back in his jacket pocket, hoping the alien would not see him rummaging for the other thing that was in there. It was stuck in a hole at the bottom of the pocket, and he almost couldn't get it out.Finally it came free in his hand. "Okay," he said. "I'll show you what I've got and you can make me an offer. All right?"

His heart pounding, he headed toward the oven. The jacket was draped over his hand, hiding his new acquisition from sight. Any human being would have smelled a trap a mile away, but how much did this space lizard know about human behavior? Apparently not much, for it didn't even look down as Louie passed by him. Or maybe it was too focused upon its upcoming meth purchase to think about anything else.

The can of kerosene was on the floor.

Louis kicked it. Hard.

Fumes filled the air as the container broke open, splashing its contents across the floor and onto the alien. Throwing off the jacket, Louie reached down and flicked the cigarette lighter he was holding. Yeah, he was gonna have to get burned pretty badly to pull this off. A couple of his more functional brain cells were aware of that. But a man had to do what a man had to do.

He touched his flame to the outer edge of the kerosene puddle and then jumped back. Not quickly enough. A wall of fire exploded right in front of his face, and he could smell hair being singed as he raised up one arm to protect his eyes. Somewhere in the distance he could hear an unearthly high-pitched screaming, the kind of sound you might imagine a seven-foot alien lizard would make as it burned to death.

And then it was gone. All of it. One minute there was fire and screeching and the choking smell of kerosene, and then there was a sucking sound, and then...nothing.

Wiping his face with a shaking hand, Louie discovered that both his eyebrows were gone. The floor where the lizard had been standing was charred black, but there were no other signs of fire. No pool of kerosene. No dead lizard.

I guess I just saved the Earth. Or something.

Louie stared at the scene a moment longer, then staggered over to the couch and collapsed on it. Now that the moment of danger had passed, it occurred to him that he might have just tried to set fire to a hallucination. Thank God there hadn't been more kerosene in the can, or the whole apartment might have gone up in flames, and him with it.

His landlord was gonna give him hell over the scorched floorboards, that was certain.

Sometime after that, a three-headed elephant came out of his pantry. It said that it wanted to buy some crack, so he told it to go talk to Duke, the big black dude who worked the corner of 14th and Main. The three heads argued briefly among themselves and then voted, and since two out of three of them found his suggestion acceptable, the creature disappeared.

Life was what it was. Sometimes you had to deal with meth monsters on their own terms, or they just wouldn't go away. He'd seen enough of them to know.

Now, though, he had to deal with real problems. Like, where the hell was he gonna find some new customers?

* * *

In the shadow of the moon the mothership hung still, its great engines rumbling soundlessly in the vacuum. On its bridge five Hsst'sst had gathered, and their wide, fluttering neck-frills offered an impressive display of rank.

"You are sure he burned you deliberately?" Commander Sz'sz asked. "Perhaps he merely wished to offer you a kerosene bath after your long journey."

"I am quite sure," Officer Vs'shtah responded. His hide was still slick from the healing ointments he'd applied, and the lights of the bridge glittered along his scales like twinkling stars.

"All you did was ask to trade for supplies?"

"I followed our protocol to the letter, sir."

The commander let out a short screeching trill that might best be translated as *Hmm*. "How very curious. And inconvenient. Our store of meth is running dangerously low; we must restock before leaving orbit." He looked at his first officer. "There are no other sources available?"

"Not in this star system, sir."

Commander Sz'sz's tail twitched in frustration. He knew what had happened the last time someone had tried to synthesize meth inside the volatile confines of a Hsst'sst starship. Scavengers were still searching for body parts.

"Did you tell him how much gold we were willing to offer?" Officer Ks'shtz demanded. "And about all our precious stones? Perhaps he did not understand you."

"*He set me on fire,*" Vs'shtah growled. His tail slapped the floor angrily.

Commander Sz'sz held up a foreclaw to quiet them both. "Obviously the natives here do not want to trade with us. And just as obviously, we must have supplies for our journey. So, since there is no other viable source of meth anywhere in this star system…"

He stared out at the moon for a moment. And then sighed heavily.

"I guess we are going to have to conquer Earth after all," he said. "Go tell the gunships to get ready."

THIS VIRTUAL NIGHT (EXCERPT)

The dragons were out in force tonight.

Ramiro tried to keep to shadows as he moved, but the narrow stone corridor didn't offer a lot of cover, and the flickering light from torches set high on the walls kept shadows constantly moving. Which meant that the evasive maneuvers they'd used to avoid the Citadel's reptilian guards aboveground wouldn't work here. If any dragons crossed their path while they were down in the labyrinth, the two of them were done for.

"Should be coming up soon," Van whispered nervously. He glanced down at the crumpled parchment map in his hand. "Any minute now."

You've been saying that for an hour, Ramiro thought.

The labyrinth was ancient, a maze of tunnels whose masonry had been degraded by centuries of rainwater seeping from above; the floor was littered with fragments of fallen brick, making walking treacherous. As they picked their way carefully over the rubble, Ramiro was acutely aware of the tons of earth poised overhead, held at bay by nothing more than rotting mortar and a prayer. *How does the gaming program do that?* he wondered. The virt software that was controlling his sensory input could add anything to the environment that a person could touch, taste, hear, or see, but what physical experience conjured such a sense of claustrophobia? What tangible sensations translated into dread?

God, he thought, *I love Dobson games.*

"You okay?" Van put a hand on his shoulder and squeezed. Ramiro could feel his friend's fingers trembling, though whether from excitement or fear it was hard to say. Intellectually a person might understand that a virt couldn't hurt anyone—it could only provide the illusion of being hurt—but it was possible for a player to get so wrapped up in the story that he forgot such fine details. The resulting adrenalin rush was very real—as was the pain that the virt would feed into their brainware if they were injured in this fantasy realm. And fear of that was totally rational.

"Yeah," he lied. "Keep going."

They hadn't expected so many dragon guards to be on duty. True, any that they ran into down here would likely be in human form—a necessary adaptation within the labyrinth—but that didn't make the creatures any less dangerous. Dragons could breathe fire even when they were transformed, and a fireball in these narrow tunnels was on the list of things Ramiro would like not to run into. But the fact that so many dragons were present confirmed that this place was important, right? That was a good thing.

Suddenly Van grabbed Ramiro's arm, jerking him to a halt. "Incoming," he whispered. Ramiro knew enough to trust his friend's instincts—Van had an almost supernatural ability to anticipate in-game threats—so he looked around for cover. But there was nothing. The tunnel was too narrow, its walls too smooth. If a dragon guard showed up now they were dead.

Then: "There!" Van cried, pointing ahead. Squinting, Ramiro saw nothing at first, but then the flickering shadows resolved into a deeper black shape on one wall. An opening of some kind? Whatever it was, it was the only option besides standing there and looking stupid. They ran toward it, leather armor creaking and weapons jangling with each step. Ramiro's heart lurched with every sound, but that couldn't be helped. When you were loaded down with this much gear you couldn't run quietly.

Dobson games were great on detail.

The dark space was indeed a crumbling archway. Thank God!

Maybe it would lead to a chamber where they could hide, or even better, a side tunnel that would allow them to get the hell out of here. Ramiro skidded on rubble as he tried to make the turn, and he had to grab onto the side of the arch to steady himself. A quick look behind him confirmed that no enemies had shown up yet. Jesus Christ, they might really make it! He turned back to the dark space, wondering what kind of chamber or tunnel they were about to take shelter in—

Only there was no chamber. No tunnel. Just a mound of rubble from floor to ceiling, where the tunnel had collapsed long ago. Despairing, Ramiro knew there was no way the two of them could clear it in time.

Shit.

He could hear footsteps coming from behind them now, chillingly alien in their rhythm. Scritch-scritch-THUMP...scritch-scritch-THUMP. Talons on stone. Heart pounding, he pressed back as far as he could into what little space they had, drawing his short sword as he did so. The weapon had a dragonslayer amulet embedded in the hilt, so in theory he was ready to fight such a creature, but he'd bought the charm from a sorcerer who wasn't exactly reputable, so whether it would work or not was anyone's guess. He wasn't anxious to test it.

Then the dragon came into sight. It was a monstrous, hulking beast—half reptile, half human, and so tall that its crested head scraped against the ceiling as it walked. Its eyes glowed red with demonic power, and Ramiro knew that if a warrior looked into those eyes, or engaged the dragon in any way, he would die, instantly and forever. The concept was terrifying, but it was also a relief; the visceral panic that he'd experienced at the sight of the creature began to subside.

It was an NP, a non-player. Some mundane person had just happened to pass by the place where they were gaming, so the virt had used him as set dressing. The burning red eyes were a warning not to engage with him, since he would not have a clue about what was going on. Ramiro watched, breathing heavily, as the dragon passed by without noticing them. Of course it did. Now that Ramiro had seen its eyes, he would expect it to do nothing else.

That was another thing Ramiro loved about Dobson Games. They wove any necessary restrictions right into the narrative, so you could stay immersed in the story. Another virt might have just slapped a cautionary symbol on the hulking figure to warn players to keep away, or maybe rendered it in black and white (an especially tacky solution), but Dobson had turned the warning itself into part of their story, giving them an in-character reason not to engage the creature. Genius.

Of course, that was only necessary because station rules prohibited multi-player virts in public spaces. If you confronted a passing stranger as though he were a dragon he might report you to the authorities, and then you could wind up in serious trouble. Ramiro didn't understand why that was necessary—was anyone really getting hurt?—but for now the prohibition was an inconvenience the gaming industry just had to accommodate.

As soon as the dragon was gone they edged back out into the main tunnel and started forward again. Soon they came to the place where their map said an entrance to the inner labyrinth would be located: the final stage of their journey. The heavy wooden door that barred their way was coated in cave-slime, but they could tell that there were inscribed runes beneath it. As Van used his sleeve to wipe slime away, Ramiro could not help but wonder at how many runes there were. It seemed oddly excessive.

On an impulse, he paused the game program. He wanted to see where they really were.

Stone walls morphed into plasteel panels. Flickering torchlight was replaced by the steady glow of lighting strips. The decaying tunnel was now a service conduit, streamlined and pristine. Wow. No matter how many times he dealt with reality-overlay programs, the suddenness of the transition always shocked him.

"Got it!" Van exclaimed. His mock-medieval garb was gone now, replaced by a grey no-G jumpsuit with many cargo pockets. Ramiro saw that the spell-chest tucked under his arm was real, though the mundane version wasn't nearly as ornate as the one Van had picked up in the virt. That was...odd. A game that could control all your senses, making you see or feel anything it wanted to, had no need for physical props. Yet apparently the box of magical artifacts had one.

As for the door itself, it had morphed into an oval-shaped portal with a high pressure vacuum seal around the edge, flanked by a security panel. Clearly whatever part of the station the two of them had wandered into, it was a place that gamers didn't belong. That too was odd. Normally a virt would never lead them into restricted territory. But maybe that was a perk of playing with a master programmer's son. Maybe the vast databanks of Dobson Games had researched Van's real-world status, and were using it to give them access to parts of the station where mere mortals were not allowed to go.

Maybe.

Ramiro watched Van trace the runes with his fingers, muttering an incantation to give the motion power. As his fingers passed over the security sensor its light switched from red to green. Probably reading his fingerprints. "We're in!" Van exulted, then he stepped back quickly. Ramiro reactivated his virt just in time to see the massive wooden door swinging in their direction, and moved out of the way.

"You sure we should go in there?" Ramiro asked. Something about the situation felt wrong. Just...wrong. It bothered him that he didn't know why.

"After coming all this way? Hell yeah!"

The doorway gave them access to a tunnel even darker and narrower than the one they'd been in. Here there were no torches, so Ramiro turned up the flame on his oil lantern to light the way. Flickering amber light played along the strands of ancient spider webs shivering in the breeze from their passing. The hollow drip-drip of water somewhere in the distance hinted at a vast empty space up ahead. Now and then Ramiro thought he saw gleaming eyes in the darkness, but if anything was out there, it chose not to show itself. Thank God.

Eventually the tunnel disgorged into a cavern whose ceiling was lost in shadow high overhead. The part that they could see was a good twenty yards across. Directly opposite them was a stone sarcophagus with figures of demons carved into its base; the columns surrounding it were decorated with matching images. In the flickering lamplight it looked as if a room full of tiny dancing devils.

For a moment the two of them just stood frozen, wonder and fear slowly giving way to elation. This was what they had come for, the prize they'd been gaming so long to find. It was hard to absorb the fact that they'd finally succeeded.

"Stay here and stand guard," Van whispered as he started toward the sarcophagus. The place seemed to demand whispering.

Ten days: that's how long it had taken them to get here. Ten days of skipping out on work and blowing off family obligations and not answering messages from friends, so they could focus exclusively on this quest. And in the end their dedication had paid off. There were other teams running the same virt—Ramiro and Van had crossed paths with a few of them—but the undisturbed layer of dirt on the floor suggested that his team was the first to find its way here. Which meant that whatever sorcerous swag was in that sarcophagus was theirs to claim.

This'll send us to the top of the leaderboards for sure.

Ramiro watched as Van opened the spell-chest and began to remove items from it, arranging them on top of the sarcophagus: amulets, herb bundles, tiny parchment scrolls...all the stuff they'd spent the last ten days collecting. The placement of each piece had to be perfect, Ramiro knew, and he watched as his friend placed them, adjusted them, stepped back to study them, then reached out to adjust them again. Van turned some pieces around and flipped others over, and then started combining them, stacking them like checkers, one on top of the other. At one point he pressed two items together and rotated them, as if he were screwing one into the other. Ramiro's brow furrowed as he watched. Van was the team's sorcerer, and it was his job to know how such artifacts worked, but the game they were playing didn't usually require motions like that for activation.

Are they real props? Ramiro wondered suddenly. Normally he'd have assumed they weren't, but the box had been real, right? So maybe the magical items were as well.

He hesitated, then visualized the *pause* icon again. Suddenly the game was gone, and in its place was a large mechanical room. There were switches and valves and pipes and data screens all over the place, and the sarcophagus turned out to be a control console. *Red ring: Oxygen,* one screen read. In the game that had been a picture of a demon. *Red ring: Pressure.* More demons. *Green ring: CO2.*

They were in Environmental Control.

Life support.

No game should have given us access to such a place, Ramiro thought. Suddenly the sense of wrongness was overwhelming. Fear was stirring inside him—real fear, not the fake gaming stuff. "Van!" he called out. His voice was shaking. "Pause the game! Look around!" His voice echoed from the cavern walls, filling the chamber with his fear.

But Van was too wrapped up in arranging his magical items to listen. He did really have props for them, Ramiro noted, but not simple physical markers. Each one was a small device of some kind, and as Van connected them to one another, tiny lights blinked in acknowledgement. The game was directing him to assemble something.

"Van!" Ramiro yelled. He could hear the panic in his own voice. "Stop it! Stop putting those damn things together! Listen to me!"

But Van didn't respond. Ramiro could have been a ghost for all his words mattered.

Maybe he can't hear me, he thought suddenly. *Maybe the game is keeping him from hearing me.* But why would it do that? What purpose could it possibly serve?

Deep within his brain, a primal voice urged him to flee. *Run! Run as far and as fast as you can! Don't wait! Go now!*

But he couldn't leave Van behind. Not if there was real danger here.

He sprinted towards the console, meaning to break apart the strange device before it could do anything. But even as he did so Van threw up his hands triumphantly and stepped back, and Ramiro knew that in the virt the sarcophagus was probably cracking open. On top of the console, the small device blinked and beeped. Too late. Ramiro was too late! One by one the red lights on the device were turning green, while behind the thing, in the real world, security screens displayed various elements of environmental control: *oxygen, pressure, circulation, air quality.*

All the services that human beings needed to stay alive on a space station.

Then whiteness exploded, consumed him, melted him. A roar like a thousand ship engines filled the room, then was gone. He was aware of being thrown back into the wall, but felt no impact. What little was left of his body was no longer capable of sensation.

Then the world was gone.

Both worlds were gone.

GAME OVER

AUTHOR'S NOTE *for* THIS VIRTUAL NIGHT

THIS VIRTUAL NIGHT is my most recent Outworlds novel. Like THIS ALIEN SHORE, it is set in a distant future where humanity has split off into numerous 'alien' races, testing Earth's tolerance for diversity. The line between mind and machine is becoming dangerously blurred, and the technology used to connect them brings with it new and unforeseen dangers.

IN CONQUEST BORN (EXCERPT)

The ice-plains of Derleth were bleak and gray that morning, as they were every morning beneath the fog-laden canopy that comprised the atmosphere. Here and there the light of a tired sun fell on some ice-formation and a flash of brightness signaled a ray of hope; then a particle-cloud filled the gap and made the celestial grayness whole again. And the sun, if anything so ineffectual could truly be called a sun, was content once more to filter its light through the omnipresent gray of Derleth and give its warmth, not to the planet's surface, but to the insulating cloud-cover.

It was a planet that truly deserved to be devoid of life. Yet life was there; not human life, it is true, but a form of being whose nature did not yearn for light or comfort. It is true that they were somewhat human in form, these natives, though protective fur covered their limbs and their extremities had evolved to meet the challenge of eternal ice. Yet they were clearly not human, for what creature of that designation would shrug at the sight of true sunlight, and praise the return of the ever-present grayness, as these creatures did?

But all this was very subjective. Azea had discovered life on Derleth a mere Standard Year ago and had not yet investigated the nature of local anatomy. Bipedal life of human proportion been known to develop independently, and perhaps Azea avoided close examination of the issue deliberately. It would be difficult to look at the natives of this bleak and terrible place and feel any kinship with them, or with their aspirations, no matter how human science made them appear. It was far, far preferable to imagine that underneath the ice lay evidence of local evolution than to believe that human stock had been placed on Derleth, as elsewhere, to evolve in response to local conditions.

This morning the wind was calm, for which the lone traveler in the wastes was grateful.

The ice-plains were not on the equator; there, where the warmth of Derleth's weak sun was concentrated, the planet was almost habitable. Instead they stretched across the western continent just south of that livable zone, bordered by impassable mountains on three sides. It took a native half a year and a tremendous amount of luck to cross the plains alone, alive. And it was assumed that no one but a native could manage the feat.

Of the twenty hersu who had departed from the mountain village with this traveler, ten remained. All that was necessary was for the woman herself to reach the far mountains; how many of her supportive team of native animals came with her was inconsequential.

The lone traveler—who was not a native—stopped to review her body temperature.

She had spent nearly half a year on the ice, cold and without human company. The latter didn't bother her as much as others had anticipated; she had never been a social creature, and was just as content to be left alone with her thoughts for a while. But the all-pervading cold of the wasteland exhausted her, and the bleak grayness filled her days with an intolerable boredom that was as dangerous as the ice itself.

I must not only come out of this alive, she reminded herself, *I must come out of this sane.*

Azea had made overtures to the fur-clad natives of Derleth, and had received the kind of response that gave ambassadors nightmares. Yes, Derleth would be happy to deal with Azea, happy even to swear loyalty to that foreign empire and offer their unpopulated lands as a base of operations for future imperial expansion. All these things would Derleth do and more, in celebration of the discovery that there was life beyond the omnipresent canopy. And as soon as Azea sent them a worthy representative to work out the details, they could get started.

To the natives of the ice-planet the issue, of course, was simple. Their own young, in order to earn the right to live on the ice-fields, first had to prove that they could master them. And so one by one they crossed the southern wasteland, and one by one found death or renown somewhere along the journey. This also must be done by the strangers from beyond the gray sky.

Since the Derlethans assumed that all societies functioned along similar guidelines—as those on Derleth did—they did not understand the necessity of explaining their customs to the Azean visitors in their midst. Each ambassador in turn was taken to the eastern mountains and shown the deadly expanse of ice, glimmering unevenly in the filtered sunlight. The Derlethans assumed that one of them would offer to make the crossing, and were confused when none did. The ambassadors, on the other hand, didn"t understand what they had done—or not done—while standing on the mountain-peak to rate the designation "unworthy."

But Azea prided itself on its diplomatic skills and had the experience of a thousand populated planets to draw on. It soon became clear what the Derlethans expected, and just as clear that only a madman would go along with them.

The Empire searched, finally finding sportsmen who would take on the challenge. Derleth turned them away. This was not a game, the natives insisted; the one whom they accepted among them must in an individual trained for leadership, not exceptional endurance. Else how could they know the Azean race was worthy of their attention?

The situation was aptly summed up by the last ambassador to leave Derleth, who noted that the stubbornness of primitive peoples regarding their absorption into the Empire was in direct relation to how much Azeans made fools of themselves while establishing diplomatic relations.

And the Director of Diplomacy looked elsewhere.

Who would be willing to face frigid tedium and alien carnivores in service to the Empire? Taking into account that such people had already joined the ranks of Azean diplomats, ver Ishte was not optimistic. But he kept up the search and at last found a volunteer, a young part-alien woman enrolled, against all tradition, in Azea's Academy of Martial Sciences.

She was willing to go; that was of course the most important thing. Though she appeared frail, her record bore witness to exceptional stamina and a fiercely competitive nature. She had been trained, as all persons in the command program were, to adapt to any planetary conditions, and to function well in the most primitive of situations. Derleth would certainly require both skills, in spades.

All she asked in return was temporary Diplomatic status, which carried with it imperial sanction. Ver Ishte shrugged and made out the proper records. The Council of Justice lodged some kind of formal protest, which the Director of Diplomacy promptly deposited in the permanent exit file. This was his department, and the only person who could order him around was the Director of StarControl herself, or, on rare occasion, the Emperor.

And so the young woman was titled Temporary Ambassador and received the coveted 'Imperial' with which to prefix her name. She quickly won over the Derlethans, despite the handicap of being a female amidst a patriarchal society, so much so that they held her back while dangerous weather passed over the plains.

She was given unlimited hersu; she chose twenty. She was offered unlimited provisions; she chose to fill the sled with the means of hunting native game, recognizing that any attempt to pack a half-year's previsions for her and the animals would be futile. She harnessed the animals as she had learned in the icelands of Luus Five, explaining to the Derlethans, when they asked, why this formation would prove most effective in the crossing. They neither agreed nor disagreed; the technique would prove its worth by getting her across the ice-plains before she starved, or demonstrate its failure by her death.

And so she departed from the eastern heights. It was a comment upon her relationship with the Empire that as many people hoped to see her die in the alien cold as prayed for her success.

If Anzha lyu sought to master Derleth's wasteland, it was as she had mastered other terrains—by submitting to them. When she lacked food, she hunted; when she was tired of traveling she erected a semi-permanent camp and attended to the maintenance of her gear until the motivation to continue returned. Neither pursuit was easy or pleasant; the game was rare, well-camouflaged, and dangerous, and to stop and rest for a day could be deadly in the cold which mimicked warmth as it lulled the unwary traveler to sleep the Long Sleep—as the natives labeled death. But it would be folly to hurtle forward and expect to keep up the pace for half a Derlethan year. Determination could substitute for endurance for a while, but in that long a stretch even determination would wear thin. She chose instead to take her time, moving quickly when she could and accepting delay when she had to. Her advisors at the Academy had approved of this approach once they came to understand that the greatest enemy along this route was not cold, but boredom.

Day after day wore on with hardly a break in the cloud-cover. Pale gray faded into dark gray and back again as the Derleth day-cycle continued. Sometimes she dreamed of death and it was warm and welcoming; on those nights she shook herself awake and saw to some menial but comforting task, such as maintenance of her weaponry or repair of her furs.

And she was alone with her thoughts, which she had not been for twenty years.

This is all that matters, she told herself. *That I've been given temporary Imperial status and that I will serve the Empire as no one else could have done. The precedent is all that matters. The people I'm serving will not forget—though the Council of Justice might like them to.*

In the long days of endless gray she did not ask herself if she was happy, or even satisfied with her present lot in life. She had learned never to probe so deeply, lest she come in touch with the layer of pain which, after all these years, was still so near to the surface.

I am, she recited. *I strive to enter the military. That's the sum total of my existence. I won't look beyond it.*

Her dreams spoke otherwise, as though the featureless regularity of the gray-lit plains had become a canvas to her inner vision.

Surrounded by the ice of her waking day, she lay entrapped by surrealistic images that stormed her dreaming mind with reminders of hungers too long suppressed, needs too powerful to lie peacefully submerged within her. They were human hungers, but they were unacceptable ones, and they had been cruelly but necessarily denied satisfaction in the waiting game she had learned to play. Azea did not hunger for blood, therefore she would discipline her vengeance. Azea did not thirst for sensation, therefore she would channel her sexual energies elsewhere. *I am Azean*, she repeated, and she forced herself to fit that mold despite the price her dreaming mind exacted from her for it. The time would come when she could do what she wished. But that time was not now, and so dreams were her only possible outlet in a world where moderation defined nationality.

Yet even those visions began to weaken, submitting at last to the ever-present gray which was the soul of Derleth. There came a day when she tried desperately to recollect the nightmarish images, to bring some variety, if not to her world, then to her thoughts. But the dreams, like all else, faded into the eternal gray, and their images were lost as the tedium of Derleth became more and more overpowering.

She suffered from frostbite, but not so excessively that it hindered her progress. Azea could regenerate what was lost in the cold, provided she survived to get back there to have it done. As for her hunting, telepathy made that as easy as it could ever be in this desolate wasteland. At times she seduced her prey to spearpoint; other times she cast out mental tendrils over the ice in search of life, but found none. *At least,* she thought, *when there's nothing to hunt I don't have to waste time and energy trying to ferret something out.*

The days became shorter. Although she kept count of them, that number was a theoretical thing; the winter-length day was more real in terms of her inner calendar. Soon the stormwinds would come and the blizzards of Derleth would slow traveling to a crawl. If she didn't reach the far mountains by then, she probably wouldn't do so at all.

And then the kisunu came.

It is curious that in the face of danger the telepath dreamed of love. It was a foreign concept to her, and not one she fully understood; whatever memories of human affection she retained from her youth had been blocked from conscious recall by that same process which dealt with her period of trauma. Certainly her recent life, filled with the scorn of her fellow students and the ever-present hatred of Azea's Council of Justice, was not the place to learn about such gentle emotions. But in her sleep she lay in another world, cradled in the arms of a man who was marked with her own alien stigma—the blood-red hair of an unknown heritage. "I know you face an unknown and possibly terrible future," he whispered. "I know you're more accustomed to hatred than respect, and have been raised to be ignorant of more gentle human interactions. But know now—and remember, when the pain becomes too great—that one man cared deeply enough for you to call you *mitethe*. You know my language. You know what the word means."

And as she reached to embrace him she awoke suddenly to cold darkness, and to the scent of death.

Kisunu.

Her mind had touched a carnivorous instinct and applied the proper Derlethan label. Kisunu—the ice-killers. Wolf-like predators that hunted in packs, and needed little food to fuel them for long periods of running. They were capable of hunting down and patiently driving to despair any creature unfortunate enough to come across them.

They were intelligent. Anzha classified them instantly with her telepathic sensitivity and was unnerved by her conclusion. They lacked any physical structures to stand as monuments to their intelligence, but despite this they could not be classed with common animal life. They had a culture; Anzha sensed she would not understand it, but there was something in them which tasted of more the simple pack mentality.

And they were very, very hungry.

She built a fire; they backed away warily, but displayed none of the instinctive fear one might associate with such creatures. Two reasoning species on the same planet? It was rare, but not unheard of.

But why hadn't the Derlethans told her?

Perhaps they didn't know.

Impossible, she corrected herself. One couldn't evade these creatures without comprehending that they had more than animal intelligence.

Yes, the Derlethans knew. And those who understood survived the half-year journey through the heart of kisunu territory.

Again she reached out a tendril of thought; quickly she drew it back, burned by the touch of animal hunger and the promise of a mind so alien that no human could hope to understand it.

Very well, she thought. *I will speak the universal language.*

She chose a bow from among her possessions and lined up arrows, heads imbedded in the snow before her. Yellow eyes regarded her with unblinking intensity and the creatures took one or two steps backwards, alert and ready. It was clear they expected her to aim. It was fortunate she didn't have to. With one motion she lifted the bow and left fly a well-feathered shaft; it embedded itself in the torso of a surprised kisunu, and evidently lodged itself in a vital organ. The creature howled shortly and fell; blue-black blood stained the snow in splotches and its death-cry resonated in the gray emptiness.

She waited, tense, for a reaction.

And they studied her. They now knew how fast she could move, and if they were indeed capable of advanced reasoning, they would know just how accessible those upright arrows were. *I will take you with me*, Anzha's action promised, *not one or two but many. Who will be the first to come at me, in that case?*

One by one they turned away from her, still wary but with their attention focused elsewhere. Each went up to its fallen fellow and laid its great teeth against that one's hide, then each ritually gave way to the next, and then to the one after, and so on until all members of the pack had performed the ritual action.

This confirmed Anzha's suspicions, for mere animals do not indulge in death-rites. And starving animals more often eat their dead the revere them. The gesture of the kisunu seemed almost designed to say, "Although I starve, I will not eat my own kind. This sets me above the beasts of the ice." *Hasha*, she thought. *Predators with moral instincts.*

She set a circular fire about her camp and hoped they would be unwilling to cross it. The Derlethans had given her skins filled with flammable powder, and now she understood the reason for it, for no fuel gathered from this desolate place would burn as brightly; the native branches which occasionally broke through the ice were good for heating dinner, but would scarcely frighten a high-grade predator.

But morning would come and she would have to move on, and if the kisunu would not let her do so, she would surely die. Not that day, perhaps, but later, when food and fuel ran out and she was at their mercy. She would have to deal with them tonight—establish some kind of working relationship that would allow her to continue. The western mountains couldn't be far off now; surely if she could buy a few days' time she could reach them.

She walked over to where the frightened hersu were huddled. With a telepath's hand she calmed them, and then with surface analysis chose the two most paralyzed by fear. They would do her the least good in the days to come and should be the first to go. With a steady hand she removed their harnesses.

It seemed to her the kisunu were smiling.

She placed a mittened hand behind each of the animals and pressed against them, thinking *threat* as loudly and as primitively as she could. They bolted forward in blind terror and jumped the fire line; by the time they were free of her imposed fear they had fallen, and the hungry kisunu made short work of their gentle but muscular bodies.

I have made you an offering, she thought, *and I'll make more if I have to. And none of you need die for this. Is it enough?*

Apparently it was, for when the kisunu had finished eating (and she noticed they divided the animals evenly among them), they withdrew to a safe distance and stretched out on the snowy surface, to nap or to wait as each one desired.

It was the first of many long nights during which she would not sleep.

They did not leave her in the morning; she had hoped they would, but not really expected it. Again she sent out mental tendrils among them, and again drew them back quickly. The hunger evident in their surface minds was less demanding, but it remained. It was only a matter of time, then. A single woman and eight passive hersu could not hope to stand against an entire pack of carnivores, intelligent or no. There might have been some hope for her through her telepathic skills, but the kisunu mind was evidently so alien that she would not be able to hold onto it long enough to establish control.

Because there was nothing better to do, Anzha repacked the sled and hitched the hersu up to it once more. To her surprise the kisunu parted before her, encouraging the progress of the sled by lack of interference. Not one to question small favors, she headed dutifully westward.

The ice-fields were smooth and without crevasses, the armor-barked branches which breached its surface exceptions rather than the rule. It was a very different place than the cracked-glacier surface of Luus where she had done a terrain internship. This, in its way, was almost more dangerous, for on Derleth there was no need for the constant alertness that kept one's mind occupied and fought back the edge of madness. She allowed herself to smile. There was little risk, now, of seeing boredom drive her to insanity. A little more risk of being eaten, perhaps, but that was in many ways a preferable death to slow torture by unending gray tedium.

"Yes," she said aloud, surprised to find herself talking. "I should be grateful to you. You've spared me something very terrible without even knowing it." And for the first me in that half-year, human laughter resonated in the ice-laden wastelands. "Such a polite enmity, my gentle escorts! The Braxins would like you." She was talking as much to herself as to them, discovering that any human voice—even her own—was welcome in the gray emptiness. "They make a ritual of enmity, and devise rules by which to control hostility and drag it out for the lengthiest possible enjoyment," She looked over the pack, a good twenty strong if not more. She had no desire to count them. "A race, then. I think we understand each other. I will feed you for as long as I can, and you'll play escort while I do. And the question is, which comes first—the western mountains or the last of the hersu?"

But long before that, she thought, *I'll be walking.*

Time enough for that when it comes.

She camped before nightfall and built a small fire, saving most of her flame-dust for when she might need it later, to drive back death. Then, acting as though nothing in the world had changed since yesterday, she slaughtered another of the sled-animals and spent an evening rendering it into its component parts. The rich organ meats she fed to herself and the remaining hersu, upon whose strength she was coming to depend more and more. The rest of the meat she flung to the waiting pack. Not enough for so many, but it was all she could spare.

"Your share," she muttered, watching the ritual division.

It surprised her, in the days to come, just how strong the hersu were. Not until there were only four left did she heed to start lightening the sled, a painful task, since everything in it was vital to survival. The kisunu could run long days on little food, and so were satisfied to lope along beside her in the gradually shortening days. She fed them when she sensed their hunger, and she fed the hersu regularly, lest they be too weak to carry her forward; herself she fed only when she had to, and sometimes less often than that. Over and over, she repeated, *Azean medicine can undo all of this.*

So she bribed the predators to keep their distance and sacrificed her own strength for forward motion, in the desperate hope of getting home.

Sometimes she slept. She tried not to, but exhaustion would beat her down until she awoke suddenly, finding she had napped without knowing it. The days dragged on without end and hunger was a constant companion. She ceased to look for the mountains; they had become a dream of the past, something which stirred in her memory, but which took too much effort to identify. An eternity had passed on the ice and the rhythm of it, chilling and regular, had finally conquered her.

Too soon only a pair of hersu remained, and they could not pull the sled without killing themselves in the process. Resigned, Anzha strapped those items of vital necessity to her back, improvised leashes for the frightened animals, and continued, determined, on foot. The yellow eyes of her enemies seemed to be filled with derision. It had only been a matter of time all along, they taunted. In the still of the Derlethan night she heard the words as though they had been spoken, and in the voice that spoke them there was no inflection she recognized, nor any hint of a language she could relate to.

Each night when she camped, she cast forth her thoughts in search of possible game; each night the ice-fields proved barren of any life outside of her own hostile gathering. If a snowsnake had moved in the distance she would have tried to hunt it, trusting to her guardians' sense of amusement to let her do so, but there was not even that. If the kisunu did not eat her they would not eat at all—and that left very little room for bargaining.

Soon the last of the hersu were gone.

"This is it, my friends." She had gotten used to the presence of the pack and talked to the kisunu with some regularity. Painfully, she looked out over the ice-fields. Half a year...it was a much longer period of time than she had thought possible; when one lived it day by day without variation it became an eternity. This is it...."

Far to the west, the cloud-cover broke. She had come to turn away from the brilliant flashes of sunlight, for their promises were empty and hope, in this wasteland, was only cause for torment. But as light danced over the ice-fields she stiffened, seeing something in the distance which had passed out of her imagining.

Then the clouds closed overhead and the mountains passed into grayness again.

She found she was trembling.

"Hasha..." she whispered, and in that nearly forgotten name was a link to a people she had lost all hope of ever seeing again. They would be waiting for her there, along with the natives, spread out in a band along the foothills to welcome her wherever she happened to arrive. It was within sight—and it was beyond hope. The kisunu would never let her get that far, and even without them she doubted she could walk the distance without sustenance.

Have you come all this way to give up now? she asked herself. *Remember that the issue is not your own life, which you never wanted, but the revenge you hope to earn. Remember that all that matters about Derleth is the Imperial sanction granted you and the influential people who will owe you favors. That's all this ever was.*

The kisunu were watching her.

Her people would be waiting at the mountains with food; that was the ultimate irony. A short journey westward and she could feed these predators until they burst. If only she could make them understand!

She reached out with her mind, and once more she touched something so alien that she could not endure the contact, but instinctively withdrew.

No.

She gritted her teeth and tried again. This time she touched a kisunu soul and held onto it. Alien awareness flooded her being, and she shook with the strain of maintaining the link. Then, with great suddenness, there was no contact at all.

"Damn!"

It was going to be harder than she had assumed. At the Institute they trained certain instinctive responses into the telepathic subconscious; one of them, Distinction Discipline, was automatically cutting off her access to the kisunu minds. The Institute's intentions were good; the Discipline was meant to interfere any time a telepath became so engrossed in another personality that he began to lose touch with his own, or when a telepath reached out to a mind so alien that any contact would be harmful.

"But a lot of good that does me now," she muttered.

She would have to override a Discipline—and that had never, to her knowledge, been done.

She closed her eyes and concentrated.

Anzha lyu was not a Probe; she did not have the ability to deal with abstract thought without the aid of visualization. Perhaps a Probe could have contacted the kisunu without damage, able to absorb kisunu thought-patterns without the need for more familiar images. Anzha lyu could not. Nor could she anticipate the reaction of one of these creatures to a mental invasion such as she was about to launch; if their minds were alien to her, hers was equally so to them.

But it is that or death, she reminded herself grimly.

Deliberately she opened herself, pulling down all her natural defenses and leaving nothing to stand between her and the subject of her telepathy. Then, tentatively, she reached out toward the kisunu she had approached before.

Again there was a terrible feeling of foreboding, and like a sliding wall, something in her mind started to cut off the contact. She struggled against it. Its strength was tremendous. but her will was no small thing. Soon she had lost awareness of the kisunu altogether, caught up in an internal struggle for conscious mastery of her telepathic potential. She held back a wall—she bound a struggling animal—she frayed a tightening noose. All those images and more, until she lay panting on the floor of her inner mind, secure in the knowledge that she was strong enough to do the one thing the Institute sought to make impossible—attempt telepathic suicide.

Again she reached out to the kisunu.

This time there was no interference. She was astounded to realize how much of that had been due to her training, and how little was due to any personal unwillingness to mindshare with an alien. With her training stripped away, she faced the predator's mind as she would a new frontier. Dangerous and seductive, deadly and fascinating—a challenge; no more, no less.

The kisunu welcomed her.

She hunted on the ice-field as it glowed with qualities she could not name, radiating heat in minutely small bits that her yellow eyes interpreted. Through her paws she could analyze vibrations from a long day's running distance, and could tell through that wonderfully sensitive tactile ability what was in the distance, and how far. Through means of an organ whose function she did not understand, she sensed the presence of life and distinguished between edible and inedible, intelligent and unreasoning, as easily as an Azean would distinguish between red and green. She found no color sense as such; what was the point? On the ice-plains there was no color, only the varying intensity of infra-red radiation which laid out before her eyes a landscape of wondrous variety, a subtle and wonderful place where the ice glowed for having been trod upon and bodies darkened to white as they died.

She did not share her own senses with the kisunu; she was embarrassed by their paucity. How could she have called this place tedious, a place so filled with wonders? Had the sky in truth been monotonous? Now it radiated distinctions of density and subtle degrees of warmth, and was as rich to her kisunu senses as a sunset would be to human eyes. Had the planet been uniformly cold? Sensory threads in the white-furred coat saw as well as felt minute variations in temperature, so that there was warmth in the breeze, chill in the still air, waves of variety pouring forth from every warm-blooded thing which one ate, or accompanied, or mated with.

She knew the kisunu hunger for what it was, remembering the feeding. How good it would be to feel that again, not only renewed strength but the ecstasy of absorbing living warmth and watching it radiate through her system—of having her own body transparent to her life-sight—of sharing the boundless pleasure of feeding with one's pack-mates. What stronger bond could there be in the universe, and what richer world to inhabit?

Motionless upon be ice, the fur-clad woman whom Azea had sent to Derleth sat quietly on the cold white plain, surrounded by kisunu. She had ceased to monitor her metabolism, and it slowed to the rhythm of the kisunu system. Her hands were limp by her sides and her eyes were closed, as if nothing she could ever see or touch would again be of consequence. She was, in all things and in all ways, silent and still.

In the distance, sunlight kissed the planet. Such warmth, though momentary, was painful to the heat-sense of all the creatures of Derleth; those who saw it strike turned away from it, grateful when it passed for the return of that quiet regularity which allowed them to enjoy the subtle beauty of their world.

At the western edge of the great ice-plain, within sight of the bordering mountains. a pack of twenty-five kisunu sat in silence. One by one they arose, and one by one turned westward. Then, as if they were one individual creature, the entire pack set off toward the mountains, under the rich cloud-canopy of Derleth. It would take them many days to get there. But the kisunu could run far on little food and had all the patience in the world; thus it was that day after day the pack drew closer to the foothills...where the aliens, presumably, were waiting.

In the distance, for a moment, the sun flashed silver on the ice-field.

It was only a brief annoyance.

* * *

Ivre ver Ishte was tired of waiting.

He had been on this dreary planet since the Academy's young student had taken on the burden of native tradition. That was…what? Half a local year ago? Nearly three Standard Years, at any rate. The Derlethans would not permit him to send aircraft low over the ice-fields, as he otherwise would have done to keep track of the young woman's progress. Since Derleth was to be absorbed and not conquered, the natives' will was law; ver Ishte couldn't take readings through the particulate cloud-cover, and therefore had no access to reliable information. "She would be this far," a Derlethan would say, indicating a point on the ice-map, "*if* she is still alive." The unpleasant thing was, he had a feeling the Director of StarControl would kill him if he were responsible for her young protégé's disappearance.

Periodically, meandering packs of local life wandered close to the western mountains. An alarm would ring inside ver Ishte's earpiece and he would hurry to the point of possible contact; then the local life would pass on its way south, or continue north, or turn back to the east, and ver Ishte would be left waiting. So on this night.

The alarm rang shrilly, awakening him from a restless sleep. "All right!" he muttered." What is it?"

A voice came through the earpiece. "Section five, Ambassador. Looks like a pack of kisunu. Apex predators."

"And our agent would be among them?"

He could almost hear the other shrug. "You said to let you know any time a large life-form approached the mountains."

"Yes. I know." Already he was rising. "I'm coming."

Section five—halfway across the length of an unbelievably boring mountain range. When he had first come to the western mountains, he had thought them beautiful: pale white cliffs and ravines, matte here or glossy there as the snowfall dictated. But if you had seen one ice-mountain, you had seen them all. And ver Ishte had been looking at them for nearly three years now.

He let the window of his transport fog over on the way to section five and didn't feel he was massing anything.

"Anything clearer?" he asked as he disembarked.

"Pack of kisunu, all right. Large ones—no young." The agent for this section handed him a copy of the readout. "And something that isn't a kisunu."

Ver Ishte looked up sharply at the man; it was a question.

"Could be, sir," the other said softly. And it's coming right this way."

Alive. If only she had made it across the ice-plain alive! Whatever damage had been done to her body, Azea could repair—whatever hurt her mind had suffered, psychic morale adjustment could handle. All she had to do was deliver herself to them....

One of the Derlethan natives manning this post waved to him. "Over here," he called, in that monotonous collection of sounds that locals called a language. "One can see them."

Ver Ishte climbed up to where the native stood, on the last high point before the plains began. Sure enough, something moved in the distance. "If it's a pack of kisunu..." he began.

"They do not come onto the mountain," the native assured him. "They remain on that which is flat."

Ver Ishte took the news with a goodly portion of skepticism. If three years on Derleth had taught him nothing else, it had given him an appreciation of how much his native guides really knew about these predators—and weren't telling.

They came swiftly, white upon white. Their approach was without shadow, and from certain angles, when the lighting was right, they were invisible on the colorless plain.

"How many?" ver Ishte muttered.

"Twenty-six," the local agent told him. And then, after double-checking: "One of them's human."

Praise Hasha! the Ambassador thought fervently.

They were clearly visible now, and if he looked carefully ver Ishte could pick out individual animals. "Is this normal?" he asked. "Some kind of escort—?"

The natives did not answer him. They had fallen to their knees.

He could pick her out now, a tiny figure staggering to match the kisunu pace. Her walk was uneven and spoke of pain—some injury, no doubt. His first instinct was to run forward to meet her. His second, that of self-preservation, kept him from doing so.

"Anzha..." he whispered.

She had come to the foot of the first rise and laboriously began to climb. Now that he could see her face, he discovered it was that of a stranger. Patches of dead skin covered its surface, which had aged twenty years, it seemed, in three. Her eyes glowed with a cruel fervor that was at once more and less than human.

She felt her gaze upon him and raised her eyes to meet his. There was suffering evident in them such as he could only begin to guess at. Her cheeks were hollow with hunger and dark circles underscored her gaze; if he had imagined a manifestation of Death, it could not have looked worse.

She seemed to struggle with her thoughts, as though fighting to recall the nature of human language. "Feed them," she whispered finally.

"Anzha lyu—"

"*Feed them, damn you!*"

He waved hurriedly to his agents and they ran back to the shelter to get meat for the ice-killers.

"I...promised them..." She seemed to be struggling for each word, as though it were an effort to think in human terms at all. She looked at the kneeling Derlethans. "As well you should..." she whispered.

The men came back with meat and threw it to the kisunu. The starving animals waited until it had all been set before them and then, as was their wont. divided it into twenty-six portions. The last they left behind as they exited, each with its own rightly earned share, seeking the silence of the ice-field and the privacy of the pack presence in which to share the joy of eating.

The young woman did not stir until they were gone. Nor did she wish to be approached. Only when the kisunu had passed from sight did she take another step forward, weakly, as if she meant to join the human company but lacked the strength to make the climb.

Ver Ishte went to her, half-running and half-sliding, and came to her as she fell. As soon as he touched her he sensed what was so desperately wrong. "By the Firstborn," he murmured, and rather than lifting her as he had meant to do, he sat by her side and cradled her in his arms. She resisted, as a wild animal might do, but only for a moment. Then, with a low cry, she buried her face in the fur of his coat and clutched at him in terror, and in need.

He held her for some time like that, sensing that this was something she needed more than food and warmth if he was to bring her home again. And she held him tightly until she could pull herself no closer, desperately absorbing the essence of humanity from him through the closeness, fighting to reestablish her connection to their mutual species. Slowly, gradually, the frightened whine which issued from her throat became a human sobbing; tears, which the kisunu do not shed, began to squeeze frozen from her eyes.

And the world was gray once more.

AUTHOR'S NOTE *for* IN CONQUEST BORN

My first teaching appointment was in Geneseo, New York, a stone's throw from the Canadian border. That's smack in the middle of the snow belt, and winters there can be brutal. So can the hours required of a young costume designer in a small college, as one has to produce all the costumes for a full slate of productions with only a handful of students to help.

After one particularly stressful day, I returned home too wound up to sleep. A frigid wind was blowing sheets of snow past my window, promising difficult travelling the next day. I decided to work off some of my tension by writing, and began to work on a chapter for my eternal novel-in-progress.

Sometimes the muse just possesses us, and we have no choice but to give her free rein. I wrote and I wrote and I wrote, long into the night, oblivious to time, until I had completed the whole story. 30 pages. By the light of dawn I looked over what I had produced, and the language and imagery of the piece resonated in my soul. This was good enough to publish, I thought. Maybe it was time to try that.

I spent that summer polishing my first novel, a sweeping interstellar tale of vengeance and obsession, and submitted it to DAW Books. They published it in 1985, and this story was chapter 11. It speaks to one of the foundational themes of science fiction: that we should not take our perspective for granted, nor assume that others see the world as we do. After all these years, it is still one of my favorite stories.

THE ERCIYES FRAGMENTS (EXCERPT)

AUTHOR'S NOTE

This unusual book requires a bit of advance explanation.

In 1998, Richard Dansky invited me to write a book for White Wolf's role-playing game, "Vampire: the Dark Ages."

According to the White Wolf mythos, the first vampire was Caine, who was cursed to eternal darkness for killing his brother Abel. Legends spoke of a document called the Book of Nod, which chronicled Caine's fall from grace, but only fragments of the book had ever been found. White Wolf had already published the BOOK OF NOD, a collection of fragments written in a variety of styles.

What Richard was proposing was a new Book of Nod, this one complete. An introductory story would tell the tale of a ghoul whose search for a copy led him to the stronghold of ancient monsters, while the text itself would be surrounded by notes that visiting vampire scholars had written in the margins, discussing its meaning. So not only would I be writing a new version of vampiric history, but also providing vampiric commentary upon my own writing, and then commentary upon that commentary...a truly crazy project. One had to be mad to attempt it. I loved the idea. And so THE ERCIYES FRAGMENTS was born.

My Caine, who allegedly narrated the first part of the book, was not a pitiful sinner humbled by his curse, but a defiant man who believed God had betrayed the trust of Adam, Eve, and finally himself. Such a hypocritical God did not deserve worship, but defiance. Caine perceived himself as a foil to the Almighty, and the format of the book reflected that, mirroring the structure of the Bible, written in the style of Psalms.

The portion I have chosen for this excerpt deals with the Great Flood. The Book of Enoch describes how Caine's undead children set themselves up as gods among mortals, despite Caine's warning that God's wrath would surely follow. The Book of Lamentations tells of the Flood itself, and what befell those vampires—the legendary Antediluvians—when the only living beings on earth were locked inside Noah's ark, beyond their reach. In canon, the Antediluvians are feared for their cannibalistic appetites. This passage explains why.

Special thanks to Paradox Interactive AB, who gave me permission to share this. The entire work can be found at their website, www.drivethrupg.com.

ENOCH

...they ruled the children of Seth as gods,
Not by man's choice, but by their own decree
And I knew then that they were doomed,
For God would not tolerate such practices.
Foolish children! You make light of God's law
But you have never seen His face.
You make light of His curse
But you have never felt His power.
He who made the world can unmake it,
He who gave life to mankind can also give death,
And He who cursed us to prey upon the living
Can make for us such Hell on Earth
That all the Adversary's torments
Will pale by comparison.

I saw the storm clouds gathering.
I felt the air grow cold.
And I knew that the time of reckoning had come at last.
The children of Seth prayed for me to save them
But I could not.
My children begged for me to save them
But I would not.
The rain began to fall, and it did not cease.
The children of Seth made offerings to their chosen gods,
Blood and gold and precious jewels,
And all the while the wrath of the one God
Drew the oceans up into the sky
And cast them down again, to scour the earth of sin.
My children cried out to me in fear, but I would not answer them.
Such is the fate you have chosen, my get.
You were gods without wisdom, and so your temples are destroyed,
Your flocks drowned, your altars hung in weeds,
And all those things which were most precious to you

Shall be reclaimed unto the earth from whence they came.
In the end you shall know such loneliness
As can only exist in a land bereft of life.
Perhaps then you will understand what I truly am
And where your duty lies.

And in the end there was only water.
My foolish children knew hunger
And loneliness
And fear
And it was good.

LAMENTATIONS

Sing a song of sorrow, my brothers in Caine.
Let your lamentations be heard in the night.
Sing of a time when water covered all the earth
And the only shelter from the sun
Lay deep beneath the waves.
Sing of a hunger that could not be stilled
Save by a brother's blood
And a time of waiting that seemed like eternity
With no end in sight.

Our father, will you not hear our pleas?
Our father, will you not answer?
Our father, if you cannot end the storm,
Then tell us by whose hand it will be ended,
And when we may walk upon the earth again.
Tell us if the children of Seth will survive,
Their warm blood heated by the morning sun,
Or if we are condemned to feed upon our own,
Sire upon childe, brother upon brother,
Until all are vanished beneath the waves.

I saw the hand of God part the clouds.
I saw the earth rise up to greet Him.
I saw the ark settle upon the mountaintop
And all the wealth of life pour out from its gates.
I knew then what our Sire must have known
When man first settled the wilderness,
And I cried from joy, and I kissed the ground,
So grateful was I for an end to the suffering.

Sing a song of memory, my brothers in Caine.
Sing a song of mourning for those who were lost.
My brother's flesh is mud beneath my feet,
The taste of his blood is cold upon my lips,
And all the works that man shall create,
From now until the end of time,
Are but monuments to those whom our father condemned.
Let us never forget, lest we earn his rage anew.
Let us never forget, lest the waters rise again.

ABOUT THE AUTHOR

Born in New York City in 1957, Celia S. Friedman inherited the writing bug from her father, technical writer Herbert Friedman. At 12 she discovered science fiction, and has been creating her own worlds ever since.

Celia's original career as a theatrical costume designer left little time for writing, but she managed to sandwich in enough work between dress rehearsals to put together her first novel, IN CONQUEST BORN, which she sold to DAW Books in 1985. By 1996 she had become successful enough as a novelist that she decided to quit her job as costume designer and write full-time. She has never looked back.

To date Celia has published 14 novels, including the highly acclaimed Coldfire Trilogy (BLACK SUN RISING, WHEN TRUE NIGHT FALLS, CROWN OF SHADOWS) and the groundbreaking science fiction novel THIS ALIEN SHORE, which was a New York Time Notable Book of the Year. She currently lives in Northern Virginia with two very spoiled cats, who insist on helping with the typing. (If you find any typos in her books, please blame it on them.) In her spare time she LARPs, plays with molten glass, and hangs out with the Society for Creative Anachronism.

For more information please visit her web page, www.csfriedman.com, or join her on Facebook to chat.

Made in the USA
Las Vegas, NV
22 May 2022

49226595R00108